Dashing ALL THE WAY

CHELSEA CURTO

For all the readers who want a quick holiday read that's more spice than plot…
'Tis the season!

AUTHOR'S NOTE

If you're looking for a story with character development, a rich plot, and emotional depth, this book isn't going to be for you.

The burn is fast. It's not instalove, but the timeline of Margo and Finn's story is short. Two weeks is all you get, so I had to write a touch of insta-infatuation for this to work. If that's not your thing, I totally get it!

A lot of this book is sexual in nature, and that's okay. Not every book needs to be the next great American novel. This is light, fun, and sexy, and while there's the hint of a plot, it's not the main focus.

BUT.

As a female runner, I'd be remiss if I didn't mention an important topic discussed in the coming pages.

There's conversation surrounding women being harassed on their runs. This is a real thing that happens daily to women across the country, including me. I've been catcalled. I've been chased. I've been verbally harassed. I've had someone stick their arms out of the window of their car and try to reach for me.

Because of this, I don't run with headphones. I tell my partner where I'm running and exactly how long I'll be. I look behind me every ninety seconds to make sure there's not someone following me.

It's sick. It's vile. It's exhausting. It's absolutely insane we have to live in fear while going for a four-mile jog. You know that post that's circulated on social media where it asks what women would do if men didn't exist for twenty-four hours?

Mine would be to go on a run. Unbothered. At ease. With no worry someone might come after me.

I think of women like Laken Riley. And Alyssa Lokits. And Rachel Morin. And Eliza Fletcher. And...

The list goes on and on.

All they wanted to do was run.

And they couldn't.

Maybe one day we can run without fear, but that time hasn't come yet.

I could spend hours talking about this topic, but I'll say one last thing: if you use Strava, PLEASE go in and change your privacy settings so your runs don't show where you stopped/started. You can hide the first and last quarter mile of your workout!

That's all I have.

Enjoy Finn and Margo and their saucy Christmastime rendezvous!

CONTENT WARNINGS

Dashing All The Way is a romantic comedy, but I want to share a few content warnings that some readers might want to be aware of.

-explicit language
-multiple graphic sex scenes involving toys, anal play, and very light breath play
-the mention of infidelity by an ex
-the mention of teenage pregnancy (and the mention of abortion)
-an age gap of 16 years (the characters did not know each other when she was underage)
-the mention of women being harassed on their runs (no on page violence occurs)

As always, take care of yourself and protect your heart. If you have any questions about any of the things listed, please know my DMs are always open (@authorchelseacurto on IG).

RUNNER LINGO

Marathon: 26.2 miles
Half marathon: 13.1 miles
5k: 3.1 miles
Negative split: when your pace gets faster as the race goes on
PR: personal record. The fastest you've run a certain distance
World Major: one of the six marathons taking place in Chicago, New York, Boston, Tokyo, London and Berlin
Olympic Trials: the race US athletes partake in to see who will make the marathon team for the Olympics
Strava: a running app that tracks your mileage/routes
Average men's half marathon time in the US: 2:02 (based on a study that analyzed events from 1986-2019)
Average women's half marathon time in the US: 2:16 (based on a study that analyzed events from 1986-2019)

ONE
MARGO

WHOEVER DECIDED running is a good form of exercise can go straight to hell.

My legs ache and my lungs burn as I put my hands on my thighs at a busy intersection. I want nothing more than to sit on the sidewalk, sedentary for the next four to six weeks, but before I can catch my breath, the crosswalk changes. The obnoxious beeping lets me know it's my turn to move, and I hate *everything*.

"Dammit." I wipe my forehead with the back of my hand. Every ounce of determination I had at the start of this four-mile run disintegrates with the stitch in my side. I never want to lace up my sneakers again. "Fuck you, Jeremy."

Jeremy Mathieson, the douche canoe I dated for six months who told me I'd never be able to run a half marathon.

I should've ignored his taunts. I should've laughed it off because I *can't* run a half marathon, but I'm a stubborn bitch, and there's nothing I love more in life than proving a man wrong.

The Jingle Jangle Half Marathon was supposed to be my chance to bask in all my hard work over the last twelve weeks, but the only thing I can see when my feet hit the pavement is my ex's smirking face when he said I wasn't strong enough to accomplish something so physically demanding.

I grimace and resume my run with new determination. I pump my arms and increase my pace as three miles turns into three and a half. Soon I'm in the home stretch, and exhaustion hits me like a wave when my watch vibrates to let me know I've reached the end of my workout.

Thank fuck.

I blow out a breath and lean against a streetlight, wondering how the hell I'm going to get through thirteen miles in two days when I can barely stand upright after four.

The math isn't mathing right now, and the last thing I want to do is embarrass myself.

"Hey," a guy in the bike lane yells at me. "You okay?"

"That is a very loaded question." Chicago's frigid December air bites at my skin. I shiver and dry my face with my shirt in an attempt to stay warm. "Is working out always this miserable?"

The biker snorts and puts his feet on the pedals. "If it doesn't feel like torture, you're not doing it right," he calls out, and I roll my eyes.

That dude probably does Cross Fit. He probably eats eighteen egg whites for breakfast and drains his protein shake like it's water. Meanwhile, I'm over here going to bed dehydrated every night because I can't remember to drink enough fluids until I have a throbbing headache.

We are not the same.

Finally feeling stable on two feet, I dig into my sports

bra and pull out my phone. I call my best friend as I walk the quarter mile back to my apartment.

"Are you hurt? Did a man come after you?" Katarina asks when she answers. "I told you to buy that knife ring and use it if someone gets too close. A study in England showed almost seventy percent of women have been harassed while on a run. I refuse to let us become a statistic."

"I only had to deal with some catcalling and a guy who told me he liked my ass. Isn't it sad that's considered a good day?" I stop to stretch my hip and almost groan at the tightness in my leg. "How the fuck do you do this every morning?"

"Do what? Contemplate the necessity of men's existence? It's pretty easy; I think society would function just fine without them. Think of how well the world would run if women were in charge."

"Thanks for the *fuck the patriarchy* pep talk, but I meant exercising. It's excruciating."

There's a pause. The drip of her expensive coffee machine makes a noise on the other end of the line, and I so badly want to be curled up with a blanket and an espresso.

"What do I tell you about negative splits, Margo?"

"You tell me I'm supposed to start slow and finish fast," I drone. Her mantra is fresh in my mind, but the executing portion of it got lost in translation. "I hear ya, Kat, I do, but *my* mantra is the faster I run, the faster I finish. And holy *hell* do I want to finish and be done with all of this. What was I thinking when I registered for a half marathon *and* a 5k before Christmas?"

"Revenge," she says, and I hum in agreement. "And your mantra never works, which is why I'm pacing you on

Saturday. I'll put you on a leash and restrain you if I have to."

"Kinky. But we should free the leash runners, Kat. They just want to be wild."

"Wild until you hurt yourself by pushing past your limits. Where are you? If you're close, you can stop by for a coffee to warm up."

"This is why you're my best friend." I tap my key fob on the gate to my complex, turning right instead of left and heading for Kat's building. "I'm thirty seconds away and fucking freezing."

"Door's open when you get here, babe."

I wince on the way up the stairs to the third floor. I don't bother knocking, using my shoulder to push open the door to her apartment and kicking off my dirty shoes in her foyer.

"I'm here." I glance at my reflection in her hall mirror and almost laugh. My cheeks are bright pink and wind burned. My shirt is damp with sweat and my scowl makes me look like the biggest grinch despite the Christmas decorations around me. "I'm going to need a towel so I don't ruin your furniture."

"It's IKEA." Katarina appears in a big sweatshirt and leggings that hug her athletic body like a second skin. She thrusts a mug my way and I take a sip of the coffee, grateful for the caffeine rejuvenation. "Please don't think it's top of the line."

"I don't care what it is because this drink is giving me life." I sigh happily and follow her to the living room. "Why do you have a yoga mat set up? Did I interrupt your workout?"

"Nope. I'm forcing you to stretch." She points at me, then the mat, and I groan. "On your ass, Andrews."

"I love being on my ass, believe it or not. I prefer it

4

when I'm getting something good out of it, like, you know, an orgasm. Not more pain."

"You're done with your training cycle and it's going to help you feel better. I promise."

"Debatable." I chug the rest of my drink and drop to the mat. I bring my feet together in a butterfly position and stretch my groin. "Have I told you today how much I hate your sadistic ways?"

"Many times. The text you sent me before you went running was *very* colorful." Katarina smiles and sits on the couch. She brings her thighs to her chest and balances her mug on her knees. "How do you feel about the race?"

"Given I got a cramp two miles into my run today, not great, if we're being honest." I stick my legs out in front of me and reach for my toes. "I thought running was supposed to get easier the longer you did it."

"That happens sometimes. You're in the taper period, which means things will hurt more than normal. You're also grumpier because you're working out less. Elle Woods and endorphins, remember? Come race day, you'll have adrenaline on your side."

"I hope so." I adjust my sock and shrug. "I want to do well, you know? Not just because of Jeremy, but for myself, too. I've spent twelve weeks going from someone who barely walked two miles a day to a person who's going to run a goddamn half marathon. I don't want all the training to be for nothing."

"I'm going to be by your side the whole way, and Saturday morning you're going to cross the finish line. Even if I have to drag you."

"That's friendship right there."

"This is your victory lap, Margo. A chance to celebrate all you've accomplished, which includes ditching that shitty boyfriend of yours."

I laugh. "He was pretty shitty, wasn't he?"

"I'm not sure which is worse: the time he hit on me even though he knew I was your friend, or the time he made you walk home from the bar alone because he had a headache."

"The headache, definitely. But that's because he never had a headache." I knead my calves with my knuckles and wiggle my toes. My muscles feel better, and I hate that she was right about stretching. "Thanks for listening to all my bitching and complaining."

"Bitching and complaining is a runner's rite of passage. That, and losing toenails."

"Which is why I'll never do a marathon. So gross." I lie on my back and reach my arms above my head. "I'm ready, though. I can't wait to see how this goes."

"It's going to go so well because you are a badass, Margo Andrews." Katarina joins me on the floor and rests her head on my shoulder. "And I'm so damn proud of you."

I smile at the ceiling, feeling full of hope and holiday cheer for the first time all day. "I'm damn proud of me, too."

TWO

FINN

"NEXT ROUND IS ON ME." Holden Spears, my best friend since middle school, stumbles out of the booth at the decked-out Christmas bar we've found ourselves in. He heads for the line of people waiting for drinks and doesn't give us a second glance. "I'll be back."

"He's not subtle at all." Rhett, my other buddy, shakes his head. "You know he's only going up there so he can flirt with the bartender, right?"

"Obviously. But being that we're such good friends, we're going to pretend like he's offering because he's a nice guy, not because he hasn't gotten laid in five years."

"Has it really been that long? Feels like I should pay someone to lend him a hand."

"Pretty sure that toes the line of being illegal, man." I tip my beer back and finish my drink.

"Bummer you're not running the half marathon this year," he says. "You probably could've won the damn thing now that you've upped your mileage."

"I needed a weekend off, and you know I like being helpful."

"That's our Finn. Good Samaritan and paramedic extraordinaire."

"Stop flirting with me. You're married to someone infinitely hotter than you." I grin at Holden approaching the table. "There he is. How did it go?"

"She asked for my name." There's an honest to god blush on his cheeks, and he sets the beers down. "I had to scream at her over the music so she could hear me. I hope she doesn't think I was being rude."

"Nah." I pat his shoulder. "There's a difference between raising your voice and yelling at her. And she was probably grateful you were looking at her face, not her chest."

"She has a nice chest," Rhett adds, and Holden punches his arm. "Fucking hell. What was that for?"

"Looking at her. You're married, douchebag."

"And my wife gives me permission to look."

"Children," I interrupt. "Knock it off. We're not here to have a dick measuring contest."

"Probably for the best. Mine is bigger," Rhett says.

"Sure it is. Whatever helps you sleep at night, bud."

I switch my empty beer with the fresh bottle and scan the bar. College kids are home for the holidays, so the place is packed tonight.

This time of year is always chaotic. The emergency calls almost triple in the two weeks leading up to Christmas. People are dumb and act like fucking idiots who think they're invincible.

We got a call yesterday about a bunch of nineteen-year-olds who set off a round of fireworks. One of them exploded in someone's face, and he's spending the next few days in the ER with second-degree burns.

My own dumbass son landed in the emergency room

last year because he thought he'd try to sled down the road on a goddamn trash can lid.

He was twenty-three.

It didn't end well for him. He ran into a post and knocked himself out with a gnarly concussion.

So, yeah.

Fucking idiots.

I used to be reckless when I was a teenager, but when you become a parent at sixteen, you're forced to grow up. There's no underage drinking or partying until the sun comes up when you have a four-month-old at home who screams for hours on end.

It feels like I'm going in reverse, having the same kind of fun at forty that my friends had at eighteen and twenty-one.

I'm not married.

No other kids besides the one I've managed to keep alive this long, despite Darwinism trying to come into play.

I have the freedom to let loose. To do what I want, when I want, and it's really fucking fun.

The people I work with who are my age still have children in middle school. They're dealing with puberty and growth spurts while I'm out watching my friend pathetically try to flirt with a bartender who's ten years younger than him.

"One more round, and I'm out," Rhett says. "If you expect my ass to get up at six to watch four thousand people run around Chicago, I need some sleep."

"Wouldn't want to hold you down, old man," I tease.

"You're older than me. Look at those grays coming in." He reaches for my hair, and I shove him away. "Are you forty or four hundred?"

"Fuck you." I laugh and swallow a sip of my drink. "I

should head out too. I have some work I need to finish, and tomorrow is going to be an early alarm."

"What are you recording tonight?" Holden asks. "Please tell me it's something good."

"Masked men. Chasing in the woods. Fun stuff."

My buddies are the only ones who know about my secret side gig moonlighting as an audiobook narrator.

I stumbled into it after the social media manager for our hospital recorded a video of me talking about the importance of knowing CPR. The clip went viral, earning three million views in twenty-four hours. The comment section was flooded with remarks like *daddy* and *I'd let him pump my chest as many times as he needed* and, a personal favorite, *suddenly I need to be resuscitated*.

An email landed in my inbox asking if I had ever considered voicing audiobooks. After a deep internet search told me the company was legitimate and not a creepy dude in his basement, I signed on to bring some of the top selling romance books to life.

Cowboys. Stalkers. Billionaires.

I've done it all.

It's been enjoyable. A hobby I never thought I'd get into, and a change of pace from the gruesome shit I see in my day job.

I've become desensitized to severed limbs and the smell of death, but sometimes, the weight of it all creeps up on you. It makes you realize how fucking *short* life is, and to not take any day for granted.

Narrating wicked hot sex scenes helps take the edge off the whole *we're all going to die one day* reality looming in the distance.

"I've run out of reasons why Jada can't listen to the books she loves. I sound like a controlling husband." Rhett scowls at me. "I don't know how to tell my wife I don't

DASHING ALL THE WAY

want her to hear my best friend tell her to *take it like a good girl.*"

"Been listening to my work, have you?" I grin and jump off my stool, throwing down two twenties to cover my part of the tab. "Maybe you're afraid for her to listen because deep down, you know I'm much better at praise than you are."

"Fuck off." Rhett hurls a napkin at me, and I dodge his attack. "You want me to ruin your secret? She'd want you in bed with us every night, reading her to sleep."

"Hey. If you want to add a third, you know I'm down. I offered years ago."

"Nope. Stay the fuck away from her ears and our bedroom."

"Already been there. You could do some redecorating," I say, heading for the door and slipping outside before he can retaliate.

I know he's just giving me shit.

The three of us have been friends for years, and we've gone through everything together—the ups and downs of getting older. Careers and kids and the messes that come with life. I couldn't imagine doing it with anyone else by my side.

My phone buzzes in my pocket, and I pull it out. My son's mom's name pops up on the screen, and I smile when I answer.

"Layla. To what do I owe the pleasure?"

"Hi, Finny," she says. "Quick question for you."

"What's up?"

"The twins have fevers. A hundred and one point five. Do I need to take them to the hospital? They seem okay, but this is the first time they've—"

"Remind me how old they are?" I ask, cutting her off so she doesn't start to panic. "Six months, right?"

"Yeah. And two weeks."

"They're getting big. Okay. My medical opinion is if the fever gets over a hundred and two, you'll need to call their pediatrician. With where they are right now, I'd say monitor them and make sure they're getting fluids. No aspirin, only ibuprofen. And don't put them in heavy clothing."

"I gave them some ibuprofen thirty minutes ago."

"Good. My opinion as a parent is that you do what you think is best. If you want to head to the ER, no one is going to judge you."

"Thank you. Ian is freaking out and it made *me* freak out. He told me to call you."

"You're lucky I like your husband. Did you tell him about the time you panicked when Jer was two?"

"Oh, god. Please don't bring that up," Layla begs.

"You took him to a neurologist when he had an ear infection." I burst out laughing. "The look on the doctor's face when he told us the kid just needed some antibiotics was priceless."

"All the parenting books said it's better to be safe than sorry! I went the safe route."

"And you're a great mother because of it. I'm sure the twins are okay, but if the fevers get worse, take them in. Please."

"Thank you, Finn. I hope I didn't interrupt your wild and crazy Friday night."

"Nothing wild and crazy about walking home from the bar at nine o'clock." I tuck my left hand in my pocket and shiver. "I'm working the half marathon tomorrow, so I'm behaving tonight."

"Good. You're stopping by on Christmas, right? Jer is coming over for dinner, and we'd love it if you were here too."

"I'll be there. I'm almost back to my place, but call again if you need anything else, okay?"

"I will. I promise." There's a chuckle on her end of the line. "Look at us. Co-parenting and staying friends after a teenage pregnancy? High five."

"We're the best in the business, Lay. I'll see you in two weeks."

I hang up and smile as I climb the steps to my brownstone. I switch on the Christmas lights wrapped around the banisters and slip inside, happy, healthy, and the jolliest asshole this side of the nuthouse.

THREE
MARGO

I DIDN'T EXPECT to get emotional at my first half marathon.

I especially didn't expect to get emotional before I even started running.

Ready to get it over with? Yeah.

Frustrated with the cold weather and having to decide if I wanted to wear shorts or leggings? Definitely.

But *emotional?*

This is a new phenomenon for me, and I'm not sure how to react.

My heart thumps in my chest as I do some dynamic stretches near the starting line on Columbus Drive. I try to repeat positive affirmations to myself, but I'm too distracted watching everyone make their way to the different mile time signs for the reassurances to stick.

"Ready?" Katarina asks me. She bounces up and down on the balls of her feet. Her blonde ponytail swishes behind her, and her enthusiasm brings me back down to earth. It reminds me to take a deep breath and relax. "We should find our spot so we don't have to dodge hundreds of people right off the bat."

"Okay. Yeah," I say, knowing I can trust her race day expertise. I rub my palms over my biker shorts and regret my choice to not bring gloves. My arms are warm, but the rest of me is so goddamn icy. "Let's do this."

I follow her through the crowd. We make our way to the sign that boasts an eleven minute and thirty-second pace, which is where I've been during my training runs. I rotate my hips to stay loose and quell the panic rising in me, listening to a group of kids belt out the national anthem and cheering with the rest of the crowd when they finish.

The race director takes the microphone and makes a comment about how many participants are out here, how amazing we all are, and how much fun we're going to have on the course.

I never would've believed him, but I know he's not lying. I watched the Chicago Marathon in October and saw firsthand what a party it was. Thousands of spectators lined the streets. They cheered for strangers and offered support. They handed out bottles of water at mile sixteen and poured shots of alcohol at mile twenty-three.

The Jingle Jangle Half Marathon doesn't have the magnitude of that event, but I bet there will be lots of energy for the next thirteen point one miles.

My emotion ebbs cautiously to careful excitement. The nerves settle. That adrenaline Katarina mentioned pounds in my blood. As we move forward with the sea of people, inching closer and closer to the starting line, I think I can actually do this.

"If you feel good halfway in, we'll pick it up and drop our splits the last few miles," Katarina says.

I nod. My finger is poised over my watch, ready to get this show on the road. "Two and a half hours of running. In the grand scheme of life, that's nothing."

"It is nothing. Think of all the hours you've already put in. Think of all the miles you've run to get here, Margo. This is your victory lap, and I want you to celebrate it."

For half a second, my eyes prick with tears. My nose stings, and I'm dangerously close to crying. Before a tear can fall, though, we're off, crossing the timing mat to a wave of families and friends screaming out people's names.

It's crowded with runners trying to find their perfect pace, but the course finally opens up as we head over the river and turn left on Grand Ave.

"Okay," I say when we finish our first mile. "This is a hell of a lot more fun than running by myself across busy intersections."

"Right?" Katarina grins at me. The white ribbon she tied in her hair flaps in the wind when we make another left on State Street. "Look at all the dogs! And the signs! That one says we're running better than the government, and that's the fucking truth."

"That one says to smile if you've shit your pants."

"You better not be grinning, Margo Andrews. I love the hell out of you, but wiping your ass in a porta potty is where I draw the line."

A laugh slips out of me, eager and bright. We sail through miles two and three, each passing in the blink of an eye. When we cross the four-mile mark, Katarina checks her watch.

"How are we doing?" I ask, trusting her to guide me.

"Ahead of your goal of two hours and thirty minutes. How are you feeling?"

"Fine so far." I grab a cup of water from an aid station

and pinch the edges so it doesn't spill everywhere. I swallow the sip and toss the trash in a bucket, refreshed and hydrated. "My heart rate doesn't feel too high."

"We're going to hold here for a few more miles. I know it might feel easy right now, but I want your legs to have enough power for the back half. We've got time in the bank, so we don't need to stress."

"Sounds good."

I take a few minutes to soak in my surroundings. I smile at the kids flanking the course with their hands outstretched for a high five. I grin and tap their palms, laughing when they lift their arms above their heads and cheer like I'm some Olympian.

"Oh my god." Katarina swats at my arm. "You're having fun."

"This isn't the most miserable I've ever been." I stick out my tongue. "You might be onto something with this whole runner's high thing."

We chip away at the distance ahead of us. The miles fly by, and when we pass the timing mat that signifies half-way, I know I'm going to finish this damn race.

"Less than six and a half miles to go." Katarina waves at someone dressed in a reindeer onesie. There's not a drop of sweat anywhere on her body while I'm heaving like my lungs are being stabbed with knives. The cold air doesn't help, and I have to remind myself to focus on my breathing so I don't get a cramp. "We're on track for a two twenty-five finish."

"Holy shit," I wheeze, fixing my sunglasses as we turn into the glare of the sun. I lift my chin and bask in its warmth, wishing it was twenty degrees hotter. "That's fast."

"It's *so* fast," she agrees. Even though she could already

be crossing the finish line instead of trudging alongside me, there's enthusiasm behind it. "You're doing something less than one percent of the population has accomplished, babe. I'm so proud of you."

That makes me want to cry all over again.

It makes me want to finish for *her* instead of Jeremy, and as we head into mile seven, then eight, then nine, every thought I've ever had about my ex-boyfriend fades from my mind.

I'm doing this for the women who have been told they're not capable of something.

For anyone who feels like they're not good at anything.

I'm doing it for younger me, the girl who never would've let a man dictate her life, and as we surge through mile ten, I could scream from the pride rippling through me.

"I want to go faster," I grit out.

"Are you sure?" Katarina asks, matching me stride for stride with her shorter legs.

"Yeah. There's less than three miles left. I can run under eleven minutes for three miles. Get me there, Kat."

"Okay." She adds a new pep to her step, and I mimic her. I up my cadence, imagining a metronome to help me keep my pace. "Then let's go."

It hurts.

It hurts so fucking bad.

An abyss of pain I've never tapped into before courses through me with every step I take, and I regret the decision when my watch buzzes and tells me we just threw down a ten-minute mile.

I haven't hit this kind of speed in my training, but I trust myself. I trust my body. I trust Katarina next to me, who reaches over and wordlessly touches my elbow.

The stretch to mile thirteen is a blur. I hear people

cheering. I see people holding up signs and yelling my name from the duct tape I plastered across my chest. I'm here and living it, but it feels like an out-of-body experience. Like I'm hovering above, the ache in my legs unbearable and the sounds a dull roar until I see the finish line.

"Holy shit," I gasp, a tenth of a mile away from completing something I never thought I'd do.

"Home stretch, girlfriend. We're one minute away. Close your eyes and go, Margo. You can do it," Katarina tells me.

I've come this far.

I've worked so fucking hard, and I refuse to come up short on my goal.

So, I do go.

I move faster than I've ever moved before.

My breathing turns ragged. My lungs burn. My vision starts to go hazy and I grind my teeth, passing a guy dressed like an elf and crossing the finish line in a time of two hours and twenty-two minutes.

Relief floods through me.

I'm so tired.

Everything hurts.

I don't know where I am, only that I want to sit down.

I pause my watch and walk toward the metal railings set up to keep non-runners off the course. I try to get my bearings, but my legs shake. I sidestep like I'm drunk. The world tilts on its axis, and I tilt with it.

My foot slips out from under me, and I pitch forward. The ground is dangerously closer than it was before. I squeeze my eyes shut and brace myself for the fall, but it never comes.

Arms wrap around my waist.

Warm palms touch my shoulders.

My body sags against something sturdy, something comforting, and I think I might be floating on air.

"I've got you," a deep voice says.

In the recesses of my brain, I think I say something back. I think I chime in with, "I'm glad somebody does." But I can't be too sure, because then the world goes black.

FOUR

FINN

THE WOMAN in front of me doesn't know who I am, but I know who she is.

Margo Andrews.

My son's girlfriend, and someone I've only seen in passing.

It was enough to make a goddamn impression, though.

I've wondered where she's been. The last time I saw her, she gave me a salute from a distance when she pulled out of my driveway and drove off into the sunset, her hair a fiery mess of red.

It's wrong to admit that one interaction with her had me curious. Had me thinking she was hot and fighting off the attraction I felt in that split second.

It's even more wrong to feel it right now when she's dry heaving into a bag with snot running out of her nose.

"Hey." I crouch beside her and do my best to come across like a professional, not like a horny asshole she's never met. My lips twitch at the look of disdain she shoots my way. "How are you feeling?"

She regained consciousness pretty quickly after she

passed out, but I was worried there for a second. Not being able to hold herself up tells me she's dehydrated. She probably pushed herself too hard, and I want to make sure she's firing on all cylinders before I send her on her way.

"How does it look like I'm feeling? Like I'm having the time of my life, right?"

I grin at her sarcasm. "I'm going to ask you a few questions to get a baseline for your cognitive functions. What's your name?"

"Margo Andrews. Today is December eleventh. I'm twenty-four years old. I can't believe people think running is fun, and I feel like I'm dying."

Twenty-four.

She's so fucking young.

Jeremy is the same age, but it sounds different when she says it.

"Some people think running is fun," I say. "And mentioning things like you feel like dying while you're in a medical tent after collapsing at the finish line of a race is a quick way to get put in the back of an ambulance."

Margo snaps her mouth closed. Her attention moves to my holiday sweater, and she tips her head to the side. "Christmas lover?"

"Come on." I gesture to the reindeer with a bright red nose stitched on the wool. "This is a classic."

"Classically cheesy."

"All right, Christmas hater."

"I'm an everything hater right now." She groans and stretches out her legs. I pop to my feet and grab a blood pressure cuff. "You're probably thinking I'm not fast enough to be acting like this. It's not like I set a world record."

"I'm not thinking that at all." I wrap the Velcro around her arm and put my stethoscope on the crook of her elbow.

A quick listen tells me everything sounds fine and she's healthy. Thank fuck. "Is this your first race?"

"Yeah. I signed up after my shitty ex-boyfriend told me I'd never be able to run one. He was some college track star, and I really wanted to prove him wrong. Guess I did. I could've done without the dramatics, though."

I frown.

Ex-boyfriend?

I've known Jeremy to be a playboy in the past. He'd sneak girls over after curfew and never seemed interested in relationships, but I thought he liked Margo. Last time we talked about his personal life, he said things were going well with her.

That was a couple months ago, and I guess shit changed.

I fucking *hate* that he said something like that to her, even if it might've been a joke. I don't know where the hell he learned that kind of shit, but it wasn't from me.

I train alongside some of the fastest women in Chicago in my running club, and they can put me to shame. Telling someone they'd never be able to finish a race is such an immature thing to say. I'm going to give him a fucking earful when I see him next.

Good for Margo for not putting up with his bullshit.

"You did prove him wrong." I grab a clipboard and make a note of her vitals. "And you did very well out there. Finishing a race is an achievement, and your time was impressive."

She lifts her chin and looks at me. Her green eyes roam down my body, and she hums. "You work out, don't you?"

"I've been known to run a few miles myself."

"Is this some sort of cult?"

"Kind of."

"Why didn't you run today?"

"Someone had to be at the finish line wearing an obnoxious sweater to catch you when you fell."

"Okay. Easy there, buddy. This isn't the start of some love story." Her attention moves to my lips for the briefest of seconds, and now I'm wondering what she would look like with my cock in her mouth. How deep she could take me down her throat and if she would gag. I haven't been with anyone in a while, but five minutes with this woman, and I'm close to asking her if she wants to come back to my place.

My son's ex-girlfriend.

I'm going straight to hell.

"You probably pull this stunt with everyone, don't you?"

Her words shake me from my reverie, and I laugh. "It's my first time being a hero. Will you be gentle with me?"

Margo huffs out a chuckle, and that tells me she's on the mend. I hand her a Gatorade and she gives me a reluctant smile. "Thank you. And thank you for saving me. I don't have a habit of being over the top, but I'm exhausted."

"That's what happens when you push yourself."

"What's your half marathon time? Better than two hours and twenty-two minutes, I bet."

"That time is more than most people can say." I cross my arms over my chest. "And I'll only tell you if you drop the self-deprecating bullshit. You did the damn thing. Be proud of it, Margo Andrews."

Margo gapes at me, and there's a glazed-over look in her eye. She takes a deep breath and grips the bottle tightly. "I am proud," she says quietly, and I beam. "I did well today."

"That's more like it, and you *did* do well today. My PR

in the half marathon is an hour and three minutes. I'm better at the longer stuff."

"An *hour*?"

"Can't forget the three minutes. Those 180 seconds are important."

"You're shitting me."

"Nope."

"How is that humanly possible?"

"The world record in the half marathon for men is fifty-seven minutes. Some people consider my time slow."

"Who? *Cheetahs*?"

I laugh again. "Exactly. Enough about me. How are you feeling now that you've had some time to recover?"

"The world stopped spinning, so I guess that's a good thing." She twists open the cap of the sports drink and takes a small sip. "Have you seen my friend? She's half my size with blonde hair. I was with her at the finish line."

"I told her to check back on you soon. The tent is too small, and they wouldn't let her in."

"I don't want her to think I died."

"I poked my head out a few minutes ago and let her know you were breathing."

Margo's face softens, and she studies me. "Why do you look so familiar? Have we met before this awkward encounter where I look like I've been dragged to hell and back by aliens?"

"We haven't met, and I wouldn't say you look like you've been dragged to hell and back. Maybe only to purgatory." We've never been introduced, so it's not *technically* a lie. I'm never going to see this woman again—especially after learning she's not dating Jeremy anymore—so there's no use in being honest about where she might know me from. Plus, I don't want her to think he inherited his shitty opinions about female athletes from me. "And I get that I look familiar a lot. I'm always a friend of a friend. Some nondescript white guy."

"Hang on." She snaps her fingers. "You sound just like the dude who narrated the book I listened to last night."

Fuck.

Her liking romance books isn't good news for me.

I don't alter my narrating voice from my normal voice too much, and the longer I stand here talking with her, the sooner she's going to know I'm lying.

Again.

Which is a trait I don't want to possess.

"Weird. I haven't heard that before." I clear my throat and point over her shoulder. "I'm going to hand you off to the dispatch person. They're going to have you sign a couple of forms, but you're free to go. We're not holding you hostage, and you should go celebrate with your friend."

"Yeah. I should. This wouldn't have been possible without her." Margo stands and clutches the Gatorade to her chest. She looks brighter than she did when I dragged her into the tent, and that makes me feel better about sending her back into the world. "Thanks for all your help." She nods at my clipboard. "Sorry about the extra work."

"Don't mention it. It's always fun when people hate on my Christmas sweater," I tease, and *fucking Christ.* She is really damn cute. Her lips have this little pout to them when she tosses her head back and laughs, and it's distracting as hell. "Make sure you grab your medal on your way out. You didn't have one when you came in, and I'm a full supporter of wearing it around town so you can show off to everyone else what you did this morning while they were asleep. Especially shitty ex-boyfriends."

"So true. I appreciate you not letting me bust my ass in front of everyone."

"The cleanup would've taken hours." I tap her shoulder and move to a runner coming in with a bag of ice wrapped around their knee. "You can do anything you set your mind to, Margo Andrews. Don't let anyone tell you otherwise."

"I appreciate the pep talk." She offers me a wave and turns to the finish line. "Hey. You probably know my blood type, and I know nothing about you. Are you going to tell me your name, or am I supposed to call you Rudolph?"

"Finn," I tell her with a wink. "My name is Finn."

"Finn," she repeats, and I like the way she says my name. "That's way better than Rudy."

With a flip of her braided ponytail she shuffles outside, and I grin as I watch her leave.

FIVE

MARGO

I'VE NEVER SEEN a place so decorated for Christmas.

There is garland attached to the wall. Lights are strung across the ceiling, and a seven-foot tree sits in the middle of the room.

"God." I groan as Katarina and I find a pair of chairs at the bar. "It's like the holidays threw up in here."

"Okay, Scrooge." She elbows me and waves at the bartender. "It's almost Christmas. Could you have fun for like, two seconds, please?"

"Fine. But the minute Mariah Carey starts playing, I'm out of here."

"Come on! She's an icon!"

"Not doing it." I shake my head, and my braided pigtails swing from side to side under my beanie. "That's the line."

"You win." She sticks out her tongue and orders us a drink. "But only because I know you're still sore."

"Sore and horny." I rest my elbow on the bar and spin on my stool to face her. "I'm still thinking about the paramedic who helped me yesterday. He was hot as hell."

"Oh! That reminds me." Katarina digs in her purse and pulls out her phone. "Someone got a video of him catching you at the finish line. They uploaded it to TikTok and it kind of went viral."

"*What*?" I grab the phone and watch myself stumble under the decorated archway at the finish. I lose my footing and Hot Paramedic swoops in, letting me fall into his arms. There's a look of concern on his face, and the way he yells at someone to get out of the way is alarming sexy. "And they paired it to *music*? My god."

"Look at the comments. I can't stop laughing."

I scroll down, reading some of them out loud. "'Hashtag: Daddy.' 'Oh my god, this is a romance novel waiting to happen.' 'Did you see how fast he was there? My man would never.'" I cackle at that one, then read another. "'Someone plz find this man??? I'm going to collapse and I need him to catch me!!!'" I hand her back her phone and grin. "Wow. This is gold. The internet loves him."

"He literally came out of nowhere. One second you were by my side, and the next he was hauling you away."

"He was nice, Kat. Funny, too. He made me laugh when I was in the throes of hell, so that gets an award in my book."

"How did you not get his full name? An Instagram handle or *something* for us to do some digging into who he is?"

"He didn't have all his information attached to his sweater, and it didn't seem like the most opportune time to find out who he was while I was trying to keep my bagel and peanut butter down. Besides, isn't there some patient-doctor clause that prevents him from ever seeing me again?" I sip on my gin and tonic. The alcohol liquifies in my blood and makes me bop along to whatever song is playing from the speakers. "No use opening a locked door."

"You weren't in the hospital, Margo. Pretty sure you can talk to the man at the finish line of a road race again."

"That would require learning more than just his first name. *Finn*. What an unfairly hot name for an unfairly hot man. He had some gray in his hair, and what was left of my soul almost left my body when he winked at me."

Dark eyes. Scruff on his cheeks. His long legs and his height—he had to be at least six-three. His deep laugh and the curve of his smile.

Everything about him was so damn attractive, and I'm kicking myself for not being more bold and asking for his number.

"Another meet-cute ruined because of miscommunication. You should've opened your damn mouth, woman." She knocks my arm. "I could track him down if you want me to. I might be a nurse, but the FBI doesn't have anything on my sleuthing skills."

"They don't, but I think I'm going to leave this up to the Christmas gods of fate. If it's meant to be, I'll see him again. Chances are it's not, and I'll survive, because he's another man I don't have time for."

I couldn't help but get off to the thought of him last night, though. To the feel of his hands on my shoulders and how *firm* his chest was when I collided with him. The man is made of muscle in his upper body, and the smirks he tossed my way made me want to ride his face.

"Hey. At least no one's in the comments saying he's their boyfriend. He's probably single."

"I'm never going to see him again, so it doesn't matter." I finish off my drink and jump off the stool, smoothing out the wrinkles in my short skirt. "I'm going to use the bathroom. I'll be back in a few."

"If you disappear for longer than fifteen minutes, I'm sending a search party after you," Katarina warns, and I know she's telling the truth.

I shove my way to the restroom through throngs of bodies. The bar is packed with festive drinkers in costumes, and there's barely any room to move around without running into someone. The annual SantaCon must've finished up not too long ago, and it feels like everyone in the city flocked here for a beverage to wrap up the night.

A dude dressed like a snowman runs into me, and I lose my footing on a patch of spilled drinks.

There's a tug on my arm and I'm pulled back, away from the olives and limes on the floor and into something that smells like apples and cinnamon. I let out a breath and look up, my mouth popping open when I see *him* holding me.

Finn.

Wearing another ridiculous sweater and grinning from ear to ear.

The Christmas gods of fate have a *wild* sense of humor.

"You've got to be kidding me," I say.

"We have to stop meeting like this," he draws out in that deep voice of his. The palm resting on my back fans out. His fingers cover my spine and reach the curve of my ass. "It's getting ridiculous. Are you following me?"

"I think you're following *me*. What are you doing here?" I sputter, lost for words as he blinks down at me with another smirk.

Goddamn him for being so hot.

"Catching you. I guess that's a thing we do. The kids will love to hear this story one day."

"That was so cheesy," I say, but my heart skips a beat.

"Made you smile, didn't it?"

I roll my lips together to hide my grin and shrug. "Can't say for sure."

Finn pulls away. He unravels his arms from around my middle and takes a step back. "You okay?"

"Minus the tripping hazard? I'm fine. Thanks for saving me. Again. Everyone would've seen my candy cane underwear if I had face-planted, and they're not as cute as I thought they were."

His eyes drop to my skirt. Mirth dances behind the dark brown. "Do I get to see them since I saved you?"

"That's presumptuous."

"Sorry. I could've sworn there was a saying about catching someone twice and getting to see their tits or something like that. Maybe it's three times. Can you fall again real quick?"

This time, I can't help but laugh. "I think it's four, actually, but I'm firmly on two feet now. There's no more falling."

"It was worth trying. I'm here with some friends." Finn points to a table in the corner where two other men are sitting. They look around his age, and they're in a deep conversation that involves a lot of gesturing. "We don't live very exciting lives, so getting out of the house is a treat."

"Is that what they call the old folks' home?" I ask, and he grins.

"You're much funnier when you're not close to puking your brains out."

"Talk about being humbled." I put my hand on my hip, and his eyes rake down the rest of my outfit. They linger on the top of my leather boots, and I don't miss the way a muscle in his jaw works. "My friend said if I disappeared for more than fifteen minutes, she'd come looking for me. We're getting close to that time, and you don't want to face her wrath."

"Why don't you join us? Not sure my friend Holden knows how to talk to women, but we can give it a shot."

I glance over my shoulder and make sure Kat is still at the bar. She's checking her phone, and I don't want to leave her behind. "Only if there's room for her too. Hoes before bros and all of that."

"Hoes *always* before bros. Bring her over. We have plenty of space."

"'Kay. We'll be there in a minute." I pause and lift my chin toward his pocket. "Do you have your phone on you?"

"Yes?"

"Can I have it?"

"Are you trying to mug me?"

"In the middle of a bar where anyone could see me commit a crime? That's not any fun." Finn pulls out his phone and hands it over. "No passcode?"

"Nah. I keep all my dick pics on a burner. You might be too young to know this, but back in my day, phones used to flip open."

"Wow. That's revolutionary." I scroll across his screen, surprised he's not reaching for the device to hide some porn collection or a whole folder of dating apps. "Do you have TikTok?"

"I'm a forty-year-old man. Of course I don't have TikTok."

That confirms he's older than me.

I figured he was, but sixteen years is a big difference.

And deliciously hot.

I bet he's experienced. I bet he knows his way around the bedroom. I bet he could find my clit within four seconds, a trait guys my age simply don't have.

Now I'm tempted to pull him into a dark corner and let him see my underwear. Would he get on his knees?

33

Would he yank them to the side with his teeth or take them off and keep them in his pocket?

I squeeze my thighs together, turned on by the thought of his mouth on me. By his proximity, the scent of his cologne, and his towering presence.

"You okay?" he asks around a rasp, and I nod.

"Great," I squeak, downloading TikTok and waiting for it to load. I find the video Kat showed me and turn the phone so Finn can see. "We're famous."

He steps closer and watches our moment at the finish line. His shoulders shake with a laugh, and I can hear the smile in his voice. "Wow. Look at us."

"Look at *you*. People in the comments can't get enough of your heroics."

"There's no hero without you."

"Another cheesy line." I hand him back his phone and our fingers brush. A jolt of electricity runs up my arm. "I'm going to use the bathroom. We'll come over to your table in a few."

"Sounds good," he says. "Can you hike your skirt up when you walk away? I'm trying to decide if your underwear has a ton of candy canes printed on them, or if they're red and white stripes."

I hum and toy with the hem of my green skirt, pulling it up my thigh half an inch. Finn's mouth parts, and he blows out a breath. "Maybe if you're good, I'll show you exactly what they look like later."

SIX
FINN

MARGO IS a lot of damn fun.

She and her friend joined us at our table, and she took the spot next to me. Her thigh has been pressed against mine for the last hour, and I swear to fucking god every time she moves, I see another inch of creamy white skin.

It's hard to look away from her, especially when I think she's doing it on purpose to be a tease, and I'm so tempted to slide my hand up her leg. To dip my fingers inside her underwear and see if she's wet.

I bet she is.

Her cheeks are flushed bright red and she keeps glancing at me. Every few minutes, she'll bite her bottom lip then drop her gaze to the front of my jeans, and I know for a damn fact I'm not going home alone tonight.

That makes me feel like I won the damn lottery.

"How did you meet Finn?" Holden asks, and it snaps me out of my daydream about her in my lap.

Margo swirls her drink with her straw. "At the finish line of the Jingle Jangle Half Marathon yesterday. I almost fell, and he caught me. Is he usually that chivalrous?"

"Most chivalrous guy I know," Holden says.

"He lent me his Maserati while my car was in the shop," Rhett adds.

"Pretty sure he saved someone from a burning building."

"Didn't he get the Presidential Medal of Honor?"

"Enough." I laugh and flip off my friends. "Don't listen to them."

"See if I compliment you again." Rhett taps his phone and pulls out his wallet. "I'm heading out."

"Me too." Holden yawns and throws down a twenty. "Anyone need a ride home? I only had one beer and I'm good to drive."

I keep my mouth shut because I want Margo to dictate how the rest of tonight goes. If that's another round of drinks together. If that's her coming home with me. If that's going separate ways and never seeing each other again.

I don't have any expectations, and the ball is in her court.

Margo and Katarina exchange a drawn out look. I don't know what kind of silent conversation they have, but Katarina glances at Holden suspiciously.

"Are you a murderer?" she asks.

"Uh." Holden pulls on his collar. His nervous fidgeting is not helping him sell his innocence, even though I know he wouldn't hurt a fly. "No?"

"You don't sound too sure. Do you have any weapons in your car?"

"Just an air freshener."

Katarina hums and looks at Margo again. Margo nods, and Katarina jumps off her stool. "I'm not far, but it's cold as shit outside. I'll take you up on that ride, please. As long as you delete my address from your phone after."

"I'm not a stalker," Holden grumbles, and he, Katarina, and Rhett head off toward the exit.

"How long are you hanging out?" I ask Margo when we're alone.

She rests an elbow on the high top. I can see a hint of her cleavage from this angle, and her intentions are pretty fucking clear. "However long you are."

"Think I'm all set."

"So am I."

"I have to be honest with you about something before this goes any further," I say, and her eyes widen.

"If you tell me you have a girlfriend, I'm going to be so pissed. I'm going to track her down and tell her how much of a piece of a shit her partner is."

"Okay, I appreciate the feminine rage, and rightfully so, but I don't have a girlfriend. Cheating isn't one of my kinks, and what I want to talk to you about involves something else." I grab the leg of her chair and pull her even closer. She's practically on top of me, and no matter how badly I want to touch her, she needs to hear this first. It might make the flirting we've done all night pointless. "There's a reason I look familiar. You, uh, dated my son. Jeremy."

"*What?*" Margo pulls back. "Are you serious?"

"Dead serious."

She takes a second to process the news I dropped, and I think it's a good sign she hasn't bolted out of here yet. Her eyes roam over my face, looking at my nose and my jaw, and I see the moment understanding dawns.

"Holy shit," she whispers. "You look… well, you don't look *just* like him, but you look so similar. For the record, you're hotter."

I laugh. "Flattery will get you everywhere."

"How the hell did I not connect the dots?"

"You can blame it on being delirious after the race. You weren't thinking clearly."

"Wow. Okay." She rubs the back of her neck. "This is a big surprise. I've been in your house. I've used your shower. I sat by your pool over the summer and I——" She snaps her mouth closed, and I narrow my eyes.

"You what, Margo?"

"It's nothing important."

"That's a lie. You fucked my son in my house when I wasn't around, didn't you?"

"Yes," Margo says, some breathy little moan from the back of her throat, and I want to burn my guest room down. "And I sunbathed topless in your backyard."

I groan at the thought of her spread out on one of my chairs with her long legs. Her back arched and her tits out. She's bold; my neighbors could've seen her from their kitchen window if they looked outside, but maybe she likes that. Maybe she likes being on display for all the world to see.

"That obviously complicates whatever is happening here." I gesture between us. "I knew who you were in the medical tent, but I didn't expect to run into you tonight. Or ever again, honestly."

"Do you think it would be weird?" She gnaws on her bottom lip, and I spend way too long staring at her mouth. "Would you consider me sloppy seconds?"

"Sloppy seconds?" I reach out and tuck a loose piece of hair behind her ear. "I saw you one time from a distance and almost got hard. Your ass looked damn good in the jeans you were wearing, and I thought you were attractive long before I thought there was a possibility I could have you. Now?" I move my hand to her jaw and cup her cheek. "I'm waiting for you to say yes. You're first in my book."

"Your son didn't know how to fuck me." Margo brings her mouth close to mine. "Do you think you will?"

"Baby, when I'm finished with you, you won't be able to walk straight. I'll give you exactly what you need."

She stands, eyes locked on mine. "Then what the hell are we still doing here?"

I jump to my feet and throw down more than enough cash to cover our tab. I hold her elbow and practically drag her to the door. The air is frosty when we step outside, and she exhales at the change in temperature. I walk her backward until her shoulders press against the brick building. She grabs me by my sweater and tugs me toward her.

There's a teasing look in her eye. A hint of mischief that makes me want to be very, very bad. That makes me want to do the depraved things I've dreamed about. When she licks her lips and tilts her head to the side, giving me access to her neck, I'm so tempted to take her right here, right now, while she wears that cute fucking skirt.

"How drunk are you?" I move my mouth to her throat and lick my tongue up her neck. "On a scale of one to ten."

"A four? Sober enough to want to do this." She lifts a leg and wraps it around my waist. I slip my hand up her thigh and find warm, bare skin. "Sober enough to know I want you, Finn."

"Does this work into some sort of revenge plan? Your ex fucked you over, so you fuck his dad?"

"And if it is?" Margo rolls her hips, and I almost growl. "Would it help if I called you Daddy?"

"Fucking Christ." I put my hand on the wall next to her head. My dick throbs, and my rationality is close to flying out the window. That's never been something that's made me hard before, but I have a feeling I'd like anything with her. "I can't fuck you here. If you're mine for the night, no one else gets to see. "

"Okay, so why aren't we halfway back to your place?"

That's a damn good question.

I could tell by her sports bra and the way the shorts she wore at the half marathon hugged her hips she has a perfect body. She's tall—maybe five-seven—and made of curves I want to hold on to while I fuck her from behind. I want to peel off her clothes until she's naked in front of me. I want to look at her until I have every inch of her memorized.

"Let's go." I pull away from her and start down the sidewalk. "I'm three blocks up the road."

"I know you are. Topless sunbathing, remember?"

"I don't think I'm ever going to forget that, Margo. It's permanently ingrained in my brain. On my death bed, I'm going to still be mad I didn't get to see your tits in the summer."

She laughs and yanks her beanie over her ears. "I wish it were summer now. I'm freezing."

"Why didn't you bring a coat? It's twenty-eight degrees outside."

"It would ruin my outfit."

"Brat." I wrap my arm around her and do my best to warm her up. "I should punish you for walking around without the right clothes on."

"And if I want to be punished?" she asks. "If I want to be bad? Are you going to teach me a lesson?"

That shouldn't turn me on as much as it does, but the idea of putting her over my knee infiltrates my mind, and now I don't want to do anything else.

"Going to teach you a lot of things," I say. "Like how not all men are inept when it comes to female anatomy. Some of us know what we're doing."

"Prove it."

I've always been a competitive guy. I'm never one to turn down a challenge, which is why seven minutes later, we're stumbling into my house and I'm locking the door behind us.

"Still sure you want to do this?" I take her purse and drop it on the floor. "Or do you want to back out?"

Margo lifts her chin. With her eyes on me, she grabs the hem of her sweater and drags it over her head. Her lace bra is bright red and pushes her tits together, and I groan at the sight of her. "What do you think?"

I pull off my own sweater and her gaze rakes down my chest. She licks her lips and grins. "What's the expectation here, Margo? A one-night stand? A quick fuck? Do you want me to get you off then send you home?"

She slinks toward me and hooks her finger in the belt loop of my jeans. "All of the above?"

"If you're going to stay, we're doing things my way." I grab her chin and our eyes meet. There's heat behind the green, and I smile. "Think you want to play?"

She's going to back out.

There's no way in *hell* she agrees to sleep with me. My moral compass doesn't know which direction to point, but I'm sure hers does.

Now that we're here, this whole situation close to becoming a reality, fucking her ex's dad probably borders on the edge of insanity.

Margo's smile matches mine. She stands on her toes and brings her mouth close to my ear. "Game on, Finn," she murmurs, and the three words rock my entire fucking world.

SEVEN

MARGO

I DIDN'T EXPECT things with Finn to get this far.

I thought we'd make out outside the bar. Maybe he'd slip a hand under my shirt and leave behind a hickey. Eventually, I'd end up going home alone.

This is a hell of a lot more fun.

The bombshell of learning he's Jeremy's dad threw me off balance, and I can't believe I didn't notice it before.

I see the resemblance in the shape of his face. In his dark hair and the way his eyes crinkle in the corners. He doesn't look his age at all, and the body he's showing off is just as sexy as the rest of him.

I can't stop staring at the muscles he's been hiding under his clothes. At his long and lean arms, and I'm not even sorry about my gawking.

"My eyes are up here, Margo," Finn says. I snap my attention away from the trail of dark hair on his stomach. It disappears into his jeans, and I wonder what the rest of him looks like. "See something you like?"

"I see a lot of things I like. You know you're hot, don't you?"

"I've been told that once or twice, but it's always nice to hear it again." His hand moves to my hair and his fingers tug on the ends of my braids. "You want a drink?"

"A drink?" I wrinkle my nose. "Why aren't you bending me over the kitchen table and fucking me already?"

Finn's laugh is loud. "We'll get there, but it seems like you've been with a string of shitty guys lately. As the oldest man you'll have slept with, I feel it's my duty to promise you better things going forward. And that starts with a drink."

"Bold of you to assume you'll be the oldest guy I've slept with. I banged a seventy-five-year-old last year."

"You're joking."

I grin. "I am. But it was worth lying about just to see your reaction."

"Brat," he murmurs again, and I'm starting to love that word. Before I can lob another joke his way, he's stepping back. Lifting me off my feet and throwing me over his shoulder. I squeal when the hem of my skirt flips up and exposes my ass. I use my hands to cover myself, but his laugh turns rough and sharp. He grabs my wrists and pins my palms to his shoulder so I can't move. "You think you're going to hide from me after that?"

My breath catches in my chest.

This isn't my first rodeo.

I've slept with a dozen guys.

Some were boyfriends. Some were casual hookups. There was a friend with benefits in college I'd sleep with before my exams. None had the assertiveness Finn has, though, and that sends a bolt of desire straight to my core.

It's hard for me to vocalize the things I want in the bedroom. When I do, some men think it's too extreme. Some say they're onboard, but they don't know how to deliver.

I've always wanted to be with someone who is sure of themselves. Someone who exudes power and confidence, and I can already tell Finn is going to give me exactly what I want.

"Where are we going?" I ask as he walks down the hall. From this angle, I have a good view of his back muscles and the shape of his ass. It's obvious he's an athlete, and he's even taller than I thought he was in the bar. "Your room?"

"I asked if you wanted a drink." Finn turns a corner, and I see the legs of a table. Tile floors and the end of a dish towel. "It was rude not to answer."

He sets me on the kitchen counter and the blood returns to my head. I blink and brush the hair out of my eyes, looking around to find him reaching into a liquor cabinet.

"Um." I squeeze my thighs together, turned on and worked up. "Okay. I'll have a drink."

My brain is already a little fuzzy from the drinks back at the bar, so I know I can't have too much. I want to remember whatever the hell happens here tonight, and throwing back a round of shots is not the way to do that.

"Tequila?"

"Sure."

Finn grabs a bottle and walks toward me. His skin is tinted pink, and the outline of his cock is noticeable through the denim of his jeans. "I don't know what my son did to fuck things up with you, but you're here with me now. And I'm going to take care of you. Give me the night, Margo. We can figure things out when the sun comes up."

"What do you get out of this?"

That same sharp laugh is back, and I feel it every-where. Between my breasts. Between my thighs. Finn's free hand shoves my knees apart and he steps between my legs, taking up too much space. He yanks up my skirt, and I almost moan as the air bites at my skin. "Your cunt. However I want it tonight. Wherever I want it. Doesn't that sound fun?"

It sounds more than fun.

It sounds like the best gift ever, and I know a more rational woman would be walking away. She'd do a deep internet search of Finn Mathieson and make sure he's not a serial killer before spreading her legs.

But that's not me.

I'm needy and desperate, and I've been thinking about having his hands on me since I scowled at him in the medical tent.

"What are the rules?" I ask. "What about my limits?"

"Open your mouth," he instructs, and my lips part. He pours a shot of tequila into my mouth, but before I can gulp it down, he squeezes my cheeks together. "Keep it there until I tell you to swallow."

I stare at him wide-eyed as excitement drums in my veins. I swish the alcohol around, and the bite of tequila melts to smooth and delicious. He pulls down on my bottom lip, watching me. After a full two minutes of squirming, he taps my leg.

"Swallow, Margo," he says, and I do. I open my mouth so he can see it's empty, and his smile turns proud. "That was very good."

I blush and dip my chin to my chest. The praise is another shot of adrenaline, and it only fuels the fire inside me. "Thank you."

"Tell me your limits. What don't you like?"

"Um. Nothing with weapons," I blurt, being put on the spot.

"Elaborate, please."

"I don't want to do anything where I fear for my life."

45

"That's definitely off the table. What else?"

I rack my brain and try to think of other things I'd never want to do. If I wasn't sitting on his kitchen counter, half naked with his cock inches away from me, I could probably come up with a dozen other things I'm not interested in, but thinking coherently is difficult. It's nearly impossible when he puts his hands on my legs and brushes his fingers against the seam of my underwear.

"I don't want you to hurt me," I say. "No physical pain. I'm okay with rough. But not pain."

"I don't want that either. Will you tell me if we're heading down that road?" Finn asks.

I nod, and it's some feeble attempt at showing my agreement. Inside, I'm distracted by so many things: the softness of his touch and how badly I want to feel it everywhere on my body. The way Finn leans forward and how the scent of his cologne invades my nose. It's all too much. Too overwhelming, and I'm close to forgetting my name.

"Yes," I whisper.

"What else? Tell me one more thing you don't want me to do."

"All this discussion about things I don't want you to do. What about the things I *do* want you to do?"

"We're going to get there. I promise." He kisses my neck again, and *fuck*. I want him to kiss my mouth. I want his tongue all over my body. "But not until you give me something else you don't enjoy."

I huff, irritated. I'm not used to being teased or having to wait. The sex I've had is usually quick. A fifteen, twenty-minute ordeal before I'm putting my clothes back on and going about my night. It's almost like Finn is making me *work* for this, and I hate that the chase turns me on even more.

"I don't want anyone else to be a part of this. It's only you and me."

I might've revealed too much with that last stipulation, because his face softens. He nods and kisses my cheek. "Got it. Only us. No one else."

"Thank you. Do you have any limits? Any rules?"

"When were you last tested? And have you been with anyone since you slept with my son?"

Every time he says *my son*, it's a reminder that what we're doing is forbidden, almost, and it makes me want him even more.

Other people might be bothered by the connection, but I'm not. They're two different people, and if Jeremy can fuck who he wants, I can do the same damn thing.

And tonight, I want Finn.

I get wetter at the thought of someone finding us in this position. Asking what the hell we're doing, and having to explain I'm close to fucking my ex-boyfriend's dad.

It's so *wrong*, but I've always enjoyed being a little bad.

"I was tested two months ago, and I haven't been with anyone since Jeremy. Nothing to report on my end. What about you? Do you have flocks of women coming in and out of here?"

"Nope. I was tested after the last time I slept with someone, and everything came back negative."

"That doesn't tell me anything about your rules."

"Hang on a second. I'm getting there. I want you to know I'm big on consent. I'm going to ask you before I do things, and you won't hurt my feelings if you're not into it, but I need you to communicate with me, all right?"

A lump forms in my throat with his considerate remarks.

I know we're here to have a good time, but I'm big on

consent, too. I'm down to try anything once, but only if you tell me *what* we're trying beforehand.

It's a huge turnoff when a man makes assumptions. Knowing Finn wants to hear the things I like makes my insides feel fuzzy, and I nod again.

"All right," I say, closing my eyes and waiting for what happens next.

"As for rules, I only have one. Condoms," he says, and I shiver when the heat of his body engulfs me. I can't see him, but I know he's close. I know his mouth is inches away from mine, and I want to learn what he tastes like. "We use condoms when I fuck you."

"Are you planning on fucking me? Or are you all talk like the rest of the boys I've been with?"

There's a pinch on the soft part of my thigh, and I hiss at the sting. My eyes fly open and Finn is staring at me, his gaze heated and heavy.

"You know I'm a man, Margo. Take off your underwear so I can show you I know what to do with my tongue."

EIGHT

FINN

SHE NEARLY FALLS off the counter when she lifts her hips and shimmies her underwear down her legs. I take the pair from her and shove them in my pocket, wanting a souvenir when this is all said and done.

I have no clue what she does for work. I don't know what her favorite food is or if she's allergic to anything, but at least I have her thong.

Turns out, it's not striped. It has candy canes all over it, and I fucking love the lacy thing.

When Margo touches the zipper of her skirt, I shake my head. I curl my fingers around her wrist and pull her hand away.

"Leave it on," I tell her around a rasp. "I want to pretend like I caught you doing something you're not supposed to be doing."

Her hesitation changes to excitement as she plays with the hem of the pleated green fabric. She drags it up her thighs until I can see her pussy, and I forget my damn name.

Fuck, she's pretty.

Bare and smooth and so fucking wet.

"Mr. Mathieson. What are you doing here?" Her legs snap closed, and I jerk my eyes to her face. I didn't realize I was staring at her with my tongue out of my mouth. "You're supposed to be in the living room."

"Needed something to drink." I point at the bottle of tequila, digging this improv role-play she's leading. I want to pour her another shot. I want to watch the alcohol slip out of the corner of her mouth until it runs down her neck and settles between her tits. "What are *you* doing here?"

"Nothing." The lilt in her voice is innocent. Her cheeks flush as she looks away from me. "I needed a minute alone."

"To do what?" I ask. Her hand drops to the top of her thigh. Her fingers disappear under her skirt, and I'm greedily watching her. "Margo. Why are you in the kitchen?"

"I'm worked up, okay?" The innocent tone turns to frustration, and I know this isn't an act. She *is* worked up, and I bet she'll be fucking drenched when I push my fingers inside her. "The guy I came home with hasn't touched me yet, and I'm going out of my mind. He mentioned something about treating me right, but I want him to fucking ruin me. Am I not hot enough? Maybe he likes blondes instead of redheads."

"He sounds like an idiot. You're the hottest woman I've ever seen. You should ditch his ass."

"Yeah." Her mouth pulls up into a grin. "I should."

I lift my chin. "Can I see? I could help."

"Do you think you deserve to see?"

"I'll get on my knees and beg if you want me to."

"That's exactly where a man belongs, but I'll believe it when I see it. I bet you're all talk."

I snort and slide my hands down her shins. I drop to

the floor, eye-level with her pussy. Her mouth parts, and I have her attention now. "You were saying?"

"Okay. You can see, Mr. Mathieson." Slowly, in the most torturous ten seconds of my life, Margo lifts her skirt all the way up until it's bunched at her waist. Until I'm taking in the sight of her and palming my dick over my jeans, hard as a rock. "What do you think?"

"Christ." I grip her leg and scoot closer. My fingers drag across her entrance, and she *is* fucking drenched. "I'm thinking a lot of things. Mostly that I'm a lucky son of a bitch who gets to have this tight cunt all night." Her legs open wider, and I grin. "You don't have to worry about me not knowing what to do. I love to eat, Margo."

I'll fuck her later.

We have all night to get to that, and, honestly, sex itself is my least favorite part of being intimate with a woman. I love the buildup and the finger fucking. I love eating pussy. Working her up and taking it away until she's screaming my name. The ass play and sucking on her tits.

I'm going to do it all.

Right now, I'm going to give her the quick orgasm she wants. She's fucking begging for it, lifting her hips and grabbing the back of my head like she *needs* me.

"Then eat," she challenges, and I love the fire she has in her.

I spread her pussy open with my thumbs and groan. She's pink and wet and so goddamn perfect. Keeping my eyes on her, I lick a hot swipe over her entrance. I swirl my tongue over her clit and hum when she moans and arches her back.

"So sweet," I murmur, and she tugs on my hair. "Wonder how fast I can make you come."

"The more you talk, the slower I'll be."

"Guess I need to hurry up so I can keep that smart

fucking mouth of yours shut." I push a finger inside her, and she's tight. Tighter than I thought she'd be, but *fuck* do I like the feel of her. "Open your legs a little more so I can get nice and deep. There you go. Doesn't that feel much better?"

"*Shit*," Margo pants. "How long are your goddamn fingers? Only my toy can reach there."

"Put your feet on my shoulders and scoot to the edge of the counter. I won't let you fall." She moves, wiggling her ass until her cheeks hang over the ledge. I trace the shape of her curves with my free hand, and she lets out a shaky breath. "I didn't hear anything about your ass on your list of limits. Can I fuck you there?"

"It's been a while." I hear the shift in her voice. How it cracks at the edges as she loses some of her power. "It would take a little to warm me up, but I like the sound of it."

"Good thing I have all night with you." I move back to her pussy. I give her clit a light slap and she jolts forward. "I'm not going to draw this out. I'm going to make you come, then I'm going to fuck you. Sound like a plan?"

Her laugh is light. "I knew you'd be chivalrous all the time. Even with your head between my legs, you're a nice guy."

"There's nothing wrong with being nice. You're going to benefit from it." I add a second finger and kiss her knee when she exhales at the stretch. "You're doing so well, Margo. So good."

She's easy to read. I can tell she likes praise, and I add it to the mental list of things I'll do again when I've gotten to know her better.

Maybe I'll wake her up in the middle of the night with my hands on her tits. Maybe she'll suck me off when I'm delirious and half asleep.

The possibilities are endless.

I spend a few minutes inside her, learning the rhythm she likes and finding out she can take three of my fingers without batting an eye. She *really* loves when I curl them inside her. Her moans turn to quiet whimpers, my name a breathy plea when I alternate between my tongue and my hand.

Having a practically naked woman on my kitchen counter was not part of the plan when I left for the bar tonight, but I'm sure as shit grateful for this turn of events, because now I get to learn how wet she can get (very). What her hands feel like when they move from my hair to my neck (incredible). How sexy she sounds when she's on the cusp of an orgasm and saying *please* repeatedly (indecently mind-blowing).

"Finn," she whispers when I part her pussy with my tongue. "I'm going to—"

"Come on my face? I really hope you will."

"I've never—this is—*fuck*," she gasps. Her legs tremble and her knees press into the sides of my head as her orgasm hits her. "Oh my god."

"You can give me a little more, can't you?" I lap at her like I've been stranded in a desert for days. Feels like I have, because I've never been this turned on by eating a woman out. I've always enjoyed it, but there's pre-cum on the head of my cock. I'm so fucking hard, and I can't wait to sink into her when she stops shaking. "There you go, Margo. Come on my tongue, baby. Let me taste every drop."

Margo groans, and it echoes around us. I push my fingers inside her again and grin victoriously when I feel her fall apart a second time. She closes her eyes and her chest rises and falls like she's been running for miles. I glance up and find one of her hands on her tits.

She's pinching herself through the thin material of her

bra, the dusty pink nipple hard and pointed as she rolls it between her fingers. I add that to the list of things she likes too and watch as she unhooks the bra and tosses it away so her tits can spill free.

"How are you—you are—" She blows out a breath. The pieces of her hair that sneaked out from her pigtails go flying. "Wow."

"How did I do with knowing how to fuck you?" I drag my fingers through her slit, teasing her even though I doubt she can give me another. "Think you can walk straight?"

"There's no way in hell I'll be able to walk at all." She stares down at me. Her skin is red and her eyes are glazed over. "Best fingering I've had in my life."

"Who knew you were such a whore for taking off your clothes and getting on a kitchen counter for an older man?" I stand and yank on the zipper of her skirt, tugging the small scrap of clothing off until she's completely naked in front of me. A sound falls from her mouth, and a quick look at her to check in shows me she's pleased. Content with where this is going, and her smirk spurs me on. "Look at you. Stretched out. Wet. Still horny. That wasn't enough, was it?"

"No." Margo shakes her head. "I want you to fill me up. I want you to fuck me until I forget my name. Can you do that for me, Finn?"

"Fuck yeah, I can do that for you," I almost growl. I unbutton my jeans and kick off the denim until I'm standing there in my briefs. "The question is if I should fuck you here so the neighbors you've probably met before could see or if we should do this in my room. What do you think, Margo? Where does the dirty slut want to ride her ex-boyfriend's dad's cock?"

NINE
MARGO

THIS MAN IS OBSCENE.

He's saying things to me no one else ever has before in the bedroom.

You can give me a little more.

Dirty slut.

Whore.

If a man called me those names out in the real world, I would smack him. In here, from Finn, they light a spark inside me. They make me want to get on all fours and stick out my ass. They make me want to have my hands tied behind my back so he can use me however he sees fit.

I know he doesn't mean them. There isn't any bark behind the bite. They're part of the game we're playing, the personas we've slipped into with the physical part of this newfound relationship, and I fucking *love* it.

I should be answering his question, but I'm too busy studying every inch of his body: the abdominal muscles, the tattoo across his ribs and the other just above his knee. His cock, straining thick and hard against his briefs, and the dampness coating his fingers from my arousal.

Another groan tumbles out of me at the sight of him.

He's marvelous.

All man.

Perfect.

The most attractive person I've ever been with, and I know without a doubt he's going to give me exactly what I want.

"What do your tattoos mean?" I ask, breaking the heavy intimacy cloaking the room.

He drums his fingers over the ink on his ribs and smiles. "This one says 'they will run and not grow weary.' It's a verse from the Bible."

I lift an eyebrow. "You're religious? I hate to tell you, but based on current events, I think you're headed to hell."

"The opposite of religious, actually. Don't believe in anything, but I like it for its semblance with racing and distance running. It's motivation I carry with me all the time."

"That's poetic. What's your other tattoo?"

"It's Jeremy's birthday." He taps the faded Roman numerals. "Cheesy, I know, but I got it when I was young and a new dad. Despite fuckups and mistakes and all the things I've done wrong, being his parent will always be my greatest accomplishment."

"Deep." I trace over the letters across his ribs. "And here I was thinking all you had going for you were your festive sweaters."

Finn laughs. "Don't get your hopes up. I'm not sure I'll get any better."

"We'll see about that." I lift my chin and tip my head toward the window. "I want you to fuck me in here. So anyone can see. Your neighbor to the left was rude to me once, and he could use a show."

"Fuck," he mumbles, stepping back between my legs.

His hands roam over my chest and down my thighs. He gently pushes two fingers inside me again, and I lean back on my elbows to give him more room. "You're a goddamn vision."

"Less talking. More fucking."

"So fucking needy." He swats at my ass with his left hand. I yelp at the sting, and he smooths over the mark with a gentle touch. "I'm going to grab a condom from my room. While I'm gone, I want you to get on the table. I'll have a better angle there."

"How do you want me? On my back? On my stomach? Can it hold my weight?"

"It's not going to break. As for what position I want you in…" Finn trails off and tugs on my pigtail—*hard*—and I hiss. "Whatever is most comfortable for you. I'm going to have you four more times tonight, so this is just a warmup."

"Four more, huh?" I laugh and lift my hips, watching his fingers disappear in my pussy. "You think you're getting that lucky?"

"I don't know. You're the one soaking my hand because you're so turned on. You tell me."

We haven't even fucked yet, but I can tell four more times isn't going to be enough.

I'm pretty sure he's ruined me for other men from that first fingering alone, and I'm scared to know how good he is in bed. It's going to do something stupid to my brain chemistry, like make me never want to leave.

"Yes," I breathe out, and he grins.

"I'll be back."

Before he goes, he cups my cheeks, and for the first time all night, he kisses me.

Finn tastes like beer and peppermint and a hint of my arousal, and I sink into the hot feeling of his mouth on mine and the swipe of his tongue. It's delicious. Toe-curling. Sexy and sweet all at once, and I grab his shoulders, wanting more from him.

He pulls back far too quickly and creates distance between us. He adjusts his erection and walks away, leaving me breathless on the counter and missing him already.

I jump to the ground and shiver. The absent heat from his body is noticeable, and I eye the table. Climbing on the furniture, I decide on my back will be the best position. I want to see Finn when he fucks me, and I'll have plenty of time to get on my hands and knees later.

Barely a minute passes before he returns, and he stops in the entryway when he finds me sitting on the wood.

"What?" I ask, suddenly self-conscious. The kitchen lights are less fluorescent and aggressive than the ones in my apartment, but I know my hair is a mess and my skin is probably splotchy. There's sweat on my forehead, and I try to wipe it away. "We don't have to do this if you don't—"

He walks to me and crosses the kitchen in three long strides. I can't finish talking, because he cuts me off with another kiss. This one is more tender. Softer and sweeter and like holiday magic. I hum against his mouth, and he sighs, dragging his thumb down my jaw.

"You're so fucking beautiful," he says, and my heart skips a damn beat. Leaps to my throat and stays there when he kisses me again. "I'm glad I get to be here with you. I'm glad I get to be the one to take care of you."

"Awfully romantic for a girl you met at the bar."

"Come on. The medical tent was our first date, right? There were drinks. That counts. The bar was our second, and now we're on our third. That's typically when I turn on the charm."

"I'll always cherish the memories we had together. Best first date ever, if you ask me. If I'm not handed a Gatorade from now on, it's going to be labeled as a disaster." I reach down and trace up the length of his cock. His eyes shut, and I hum. "You tortured me, Finn. Maybe it's time I torture you."

"It would be worth it." Finn blows out a heavy exhale and his breath ghosts over my skin. He rips open the condom wrapper with his teeth and his hand drops between my legs. "Still wet for me, baby?"

I usually *hate* pet names in bed. They make me cringe and roll my eyes, but like everything else tonight, it's different with Finn.

There's a hint of teasing behind it. A dash of reverence that tells me this might be a quick fling, something we'll both forget about by the time the clock strikes midnight on New Year's Eve, but that there's a world out there where it could've existed as something more substantial and profound.

"Check for yourself," I say, but the words get tangled when he slowly pushes his fingers inside me. When he rests his other hand on my stomach and chuckles in some sly, sexy way as he drops his forehead against mine.

"Yeah, you are. Do you get this wet for other guys, Margo? Or is it just me?"

"Just you," I tell him, and it's the damn truth.

I've had orgasms. Guys have gotten me off. But I've never felt like *this*, like I'm simultaneously on top of the world but also rooted to him. Everything is magnified; his touch is electric. His words are poetic, and his mouth soothes every ache I've ever had.

It's been a rush up to this point, and for as much as I want him to fuck me hard and rough, I want him to savor me too. To go slow, so I enjoy every second of bliss he's going to bring me.

"Good answer." Finn drops his hands away and

strokes his cock. He slides the condom down his length and his eyes glint with excitement when he grabs the underside of my thighs and hauls me toward him. "You ready, Margo?"

I tip my head to the side and kiss him. My teeth bite at his lower lip and my tongue glides against his. He grunts and grips my legs even harder, the press of his fingers rough enough to leave behind marks I'm going to wear around like a trophy tomorrow.

"Fuck me, Finn," I whisper, and he lines up with my entrance.

He runs the head of his cock against my pussy, teasing me, and I see how wet I am. I plant my hands on the table to stabilize myself and dig my nails into the wood as he rocks forward and buries the first half of his length inside me with a slick and easy glide.

"*Fuck*," we say in unison.

My breath gets stuck behind my ribs. His head drops back and his throat bobs. A bead of sweat rolls down his arm, and I don't know if I want him to move or stay still so I can get used to the stretch.

"*Jesus*. How are you this fucking tight? I worked your cunt for ten minutes and it's like you've never been touched." Finn snaps his hips, and another inch of his long cock disappears inside me. I try to say something, but the words don't come out. I'm so *full*, and he's not even all the way in yet. "Perfect." He thrusts again. "Fucking." Another inch deeper. "Pussy."

I swear I levitate off the table when he fully buries himself in me. The rush of pain is quick and fleeting before it subsides to something pleasurable. Something magnificent as our bodies join and there's no space to know where he ends and I begin.

"Harder," I gasp. I keep my eyes on his as he stares

right back at me. "I can take more. I *want* more, Mr. Mathieson."

I've never been into role-playing either, but drawing attention to the fact I *shouldn't* be clenching around his cock while he's balls deep in my pussy makes this whole situation even hotter. Makes me even wetter, and I palm his ass, urging him forward, as if the eight inches he's fucking me with aren't enough.

"Dirty girl," he whispers in my ear. "Tell me, Margo. If I had been here when you and Jeremy were using my pool over the summer, would you have come and found me? Would you have slipped into my bedroom while your boyfriend was in the kitchen and showed off your body? Would you have taunted me with what I couldn't have?" Finn twists my nipple, and I cry out. "Maybe this was your plan all along."

It wasn't.

Nothing about my time with him has been planned or calculated, but I wish it was. I imagine sneaking down the hall. Finding him in his room and locking the door behind me as I dropped to my knees and sucked him off, all while my piece of shit ex sat clueless mere feet away.

The fantasy is dirty and wrong. It turns impossibly filthy when I picture him spreading me out on his bed and going down on me, forcing me to be quiet with a large hand over my mouth so no one overhears the way he makes me feel so damn *good*.

"What are you thinking about?" Finn asks. "You just clenched around me. You're almost milking my cock, Margo, so it must be fucking filthy."

"You. And doing things we shouldn't."

"Like?"

"Like giving you a blow job with Jeremy in the other room," I admit, and he touches my neck. Strokes his thumb down my throat, and I groan. "It's a shame we only have tonight. That could've been fun."

He slams into me, and I see stars. His movements turn unhinged, almost, and I imagine he's losing his mind, just like I am. "I sure hope my neighbors are watching."

A laugh sneaks out of me at the same time he presses on my clit with his thumb, and it drops to a strangled whine. "More," I beg. "Want to come on your cock, Finn."

"Am I doing this right, Margo?" Finn folds my knees to my chest and brings my legs together. He pulls out of me, and I squirm, empty without him. There's a second of teasing. Of watching him drag his cock over the inside of my thighs, marking me with my arousal as he tuts and shakes his head. My skin burns at the indifference on his face, a man on a mission to make a mess of me. "Is this good enough for the woman who begged me to take her home?"

"Finn," I pant.

He taps the head of his cock against my clit. When I try to open my knees so he can fuck me again, he gives my breast a light slap. "You didn't answer my question."

"Yes. *Yes*. Of course it's good enough," I say, angry that he's keeping me waiting. Angry at how badly I want him. Angry that I haven't gotten a third orgasm yet. "Can you let me come, please?"

"Only because you asked so nicely." He drags his hands up my thigh and holds my legs open. "And only if you say my name when you do."

I don't have time to argue, because he's filling me up again. Taking the space where he was before and pushing me to the brink of ecstasy with bruising and rough thrusts. I close my eyes and reach for it, the intense satisfaction of being thoroughly fucked building at the base of my spine.

Everything is a blur. I hear his grunts and feel his hands

touching me everywhere he can reach. I can smell the peppermint on the tip of his tongue, and when he pinches my nipple, I fall apart.

I think I say Finn's name. I'm not sure, because my body is weightless as he works me down from the orgasm that tears through me. I tremble and shake, my limbs tired and heavy when I finally open my eyes and blink up at him.

"Okay?" Finn asks, still hard and buried inside me.

"Yeah." I swallow and take a deep breath. "Did you come?"

"Not yet. Wanted to get you there first."

"Of course you did." I circle my hips and he almost falls forward. "Oh, did you like that, Mr. Mathieson?"

"*Christ*, Margo. Do that again. Please," he says, and I grin.

"I like it when you beg." I move my hips again, delighted when he puts one hand on the table. I wrap my legs around his waist and work up and down his cock, using the leverage from the table to get him nice and deep. "Are you going to come inside me?"

"Yes," he hisses. "Just—right there. That's—"

Finn snaps his hips into mine as he loses himself. His own orgasm hits him and he groans, the sound masculine and sharp. His movements slow and his hold on me loosens until he's folding his body over mine, looking thoroughly spent.

"Hey," I whisper, and his eyes sparkle with glee. "You doing okay, old man?"

"I'm going to put you over my fucking knee later," he warns me.

I grin. "Told you I wanted to be punished."

"Christ." He shakes his head. "I think you might kill me tonight."

"There are worse ways to go, aren't there?"

"Besides your pussy or with my hands on your ass? Definitely." Finn grimaces and pulls his softening cock out of me. "Fucking hell. I could spend forever there."

"Probably the most interesting compliment I've gotten, but I'll take it." I prop myself up on my elbows. "That was enjoyable."

"Enjoyable," he repeats with a laugh. "Better than terrible, I guess."

"You know nothing about that was terrible."

"Yeah." His eyes meet mine, and he smiles. "I do know that."

I clear my throat, not sure what comes next. We agreed this would be for the night, but that was before he fucked me. In the aftermath, I don't know how he wants this to go.

"Do you... should I..." I trail off and wonder where my clothes ended up. "I can—"

"The only place you're going is the shower so I can clean you up before having you again." Finn scoops me into his arms like I weigh absolutely nothing and walks us down the hall. "You've got a long night ahead of you, Margo."

TEN

MARGO

I WAKE up warm and buried under a pile of blankets. I groan and I stretch my arms above my head, sore and tired after spending all night with Finn. He was true to his word, having me three more times while the stars were out and again just as the sun started to rise. I flip onto my side, ready to wake him up with my mouth on his cock, but I frown when I find the space beside me empty.

That's not good.

I sit up and glance around. There are no signs of life in his bedroom except for a sticky note attached to his pillow. I grab it off the silk fabric and read it, my frown pulling up into a smile when I see his messy handwriting.

> You snore in your sleep.
> Come to the kitchen when you wake up.
> Fa-la-la-la Finn

There's even a damn reindeer next to his name.

I throw back the covers and jump out of bed, finding a

big T-shirt of his to slip on. I make my way over to the dresser against the wall and put on a pair of fuzzy socks, grateful the central heat is kicking out most of the cold in the room.

Opening the door, I pad down the hall and grin when I see an eight-foot Christmas tree in the living room. It's decorated from top to bottom with ornaments and colored lights, and I walk over to smell the fresh pine needles.

The few times I've been to his house with Jeremy, I haven't taken a good look around. We've usually headed out to the pool or stayed in the kitchen to grab a bite to eat, so I take a second to admire the area around me.

A quick scan shows me he has a matching couch and loveseat set. A fancy coffee table in the middle of the room and a bookshelf against the wall that's covered in garland.

Everything about it is adult and mature, a guy who obviously has his shit together, but I'm not surprised. The man has a headboard, for god's sake, so a fully furnished house isn't a shock.

Tapping one of the lights, I veer left toward the kitchen and find Finn bent over the stove. His sweatpants sit low on his hips, and there are red marks all over his shoulders from where my nails dug into his skin when we went for round two in his bedroom. I cross my arms over my chest and watch him for a minute.

He knows his way around a kitchen, flipping a pancake and cracking an egg like he's a Michelin star chef. I hear him humming a low tune, and I wonder what he's singing.

"Morning," I say, announcing my presence.

Finn turns to look at me over his shoulder. His eyes move down my shirt and bare legs, and a slow and lazy grin stretches across his mouth.

"Morning."

I yawn and step into the kitchen. "Do you have coffee?"

"Just brewed a fresh pot. The only things I know about you are how many of my fingers you can take and that you steal the covers in the night, so I wasn't sure if you wanted milk and sugar."

I burst out laughing and take the mug he's handing me. It's covered in snowflakes, and the man might as well be Santa Claus himself. "While those are important things, coffee is *more* important. Splash of milk, half a spoonful of sugar."

"Noted. Help yourself to anything. Food should be ready in five minutes."

"That's all right. I don't want to linger, and I'm sure you want to get back into your routine. Once I finish this, I'm going to head out."

"Head out?" Finn chuckles. "Blizzard came through last night, and it's still coming down. The streets are closed, so there's no way you'll find an Uber."

"What?" I stand on my toes and pull back the small curtain covering the window above the kitchen sink. It's a world of white outside, and I stare at the snow piling up, knowing there's no way I'm going to make it home in the foreseeable future. "That derails my plans."

"Why don't you eat and hang out for a while? When it clears, I can either drive you home or call a car for you."

"I don't want to be in your way."

"You won't be."

I deliberate for a beat before conceding. I didn't expect to interact with him once the day started, but I might as well take advantage of the situation. "The second it stops snowing I'm going to leave."

"That's fine."

I pull out a chair at the table and sit. "Do you like to cook?"

"I don't mind it. I eat a lot when I'm marathon training, so making my meals is a lot cheaper than going out. That shit adds up," Finn says.

"How many marathons have you done?" I ask, watching him dole out food onto two plates.

"Seven."

"And you're fast, right?"

"I guess you could say that. I finished eighth at the Olympic Trials in the marathon this year."

"*What*? You're joking."

"Nope." He sets the plates down and sits across from me. "I like to run."

"My god. You must've thought I was absolutely ridiculous acting like that after a half marathon."

"I told you I don't think that way. We all have different abilities, and I bet I've been running far longer than you."

"Probably longer than I've been alive," I say under my breath, and he reaches under the table and squeezes my knee.

"You're not wrong. Now eat, Margo, and tell me how you slept."

"Pretty well." I cut a piece of pancake and swallow it down. "Your bed is very comfortable."

"It is, isn't it? I splurged on it a couple of years ago, and it's done wonders for my back problems." Finn spears his scrambled eggs and shovels a bite into his mouth with a smile. "What do you do for work?"

"Are we playing the Twenty Questions game?"

"We might as well. This is our fourth date, after all."

"I'm not sure I've ever had a guy want to get to know me after he fucked me." I take a swig of my coffee and sigh happily. "I'm a third-grade teacher. We're off until the new year and having some time away from the classroom is a treat."

"A teacher? That's awesome. How'd you get into that gig?" he asks.

"You make it sound like I work for the FBI, not molding the minds of the next generation of leaders. But, yes, to answer your question: I got my degree in biology, only I didn't want to spend all day in a lab, so I went the teaching route. Once I feel more comfortable in a classroom environment, I want to transition to high school. The younger kids are fun, but it requires *a lot* of patience."

"Teachers are superheroes. My mom was in education for thirty-five years, and I have immense respect for what you do. I'd probably get fired after ten minutes, and I'm definitely not smart enough to inspire young minds."

"I don't know about that. A lot of it is a curriculum that's given to you. This is my third year, and I'm finally at the point where I think I know what I'm doing." I glance up at him. "You're a paramedic, right? Or some kind of doctor?"

"Paramedic. Been in the field for about ten years now, and I love it."

"You must see a lot of shit."

"I do," he says. "But I bet you do too."

"I'm not performing CPR on my students."

"Maybe not. But you do see how tired they are after they've listened to their parents fight all night. You see them skipping meals and experiencing emotions that are tough to work through when you're young. That can have similar weight to the stuff I deal with."

He's not wrong.

What I do is 30 percent teaching, 70 percent listening, observing, helping and loving. I have kids from broken homes. Kids who didn't eat dinner last night. Others who are three reading levels behind because they don't have an adult in their life who believes in them.

For as much as I love my job, there's a lot of heartbreak too, and this is the first time someone's sounded so understanding when talking about the challenges I face in my profession.

"I guess you're right," I say, rubbing a hand over my chest. "Still. What you do is more important."

"We're both important," Finn says.

"Okay, humble guy. You win. We're both important. My turn for a question?"

"Sure. I'm an open book. Ask whatever you want."

"What's the deal with Jeremy's mom? Is she still in the picture? I know what happened between us doesn't mean anything when I leave, but is she going to come through the door in an hour and want to kick my ass for sleeping with you?"

"That would be awkward, given she has six-month-old twins and a husband she loves very much. We had Jeremy when we were young. Sixteen, juniors in high school, and really fucking clueless. It happened after the homecoming dance. I wanted to make the night romantic, so we drove out to this open field and looked at the stars." He grins and leans back in his chair. "We didn't know any better, and a few weeks later, she missed her period. I told her I'd support her no matter what she decided to do: keep the baby, have an abortion, place him up for adoption. Ultimately, she decided to keep it, and Jeremy was born."

"Okay, so that was twenty-something years ago. What about now?"

"We dated until we graduated college. After, we parted ways as partners but stayed friends. We love each other, but we're not in love with each other, if that makes sense."

"Makes total sense. How was it co-parenting?"

"So easy, but I know not everyone can say the same. Layla and I always communicated with one another. We split custody of Jer, and there was never any drama. We had a good support system, and we both sacrificed a lot for him." He pauses, and the weight of his gaze is heavy on my shoulders. "What happened between you two? He mentioned you a few times, but he didn't mention a breakup."

I take a bite of food to give myself a second before answering. "He cheated on me," I say bluntly when I swallow, and Finn's eyes widen.

"*What?*"

"We were out at a bar and he said he wasn't feeling well, so he wanted to head home. He wasn't answering my texts when I asked if he got back okay, and I saw he was still sharing his location with me from earlier in the day. Turns out, he went to the restaurant next door where he was meeting up with the woman who teaches in the classroom next to mine. They were going at it in the bathroom." I laugh. The whole thing sounds absolutely ridiculous now. "He's a piece of shit. Sorry. I know he's your son and what we had wasn't that serious, but a little decency would've been nice."

"Fucking Christ." Finn pinches the bridge of his nose and shakes his head. "I'm sorry, Margo. I don't know where he learned that shit, but it wasn't from me."

"It's fine. I knew I wasn't going to marry the guy. Just, you know, I'd rather not have seen my boyfriend's mouth on another woman."

"Still. That's unacceptable. It's not hard to have a conversation with the person you've been seeing and tell them you're not interested in pursuing things with them anymore."

"It's no big deal. If we hadn't broken up, I wouldn't be

here right now, and I'm having a lot of fun. You're putting me in the holiday spirit with your tree and decorations, and I'm forgetting all about him."

"It's Christmas, Margo. Everyone should be in the holiday spirit."

We make casual conversation for the rest of our meal. Finn tells me about growing up just outside of Chicago in a small suburb. I tell him about my childhood and my sixth-grade science fair project.

Everything about it is easy. I can't stop laughing, and there's not an ounce of awkwardness in hanging out like friends after he railed me for hours last night.

"So." I wipe my mouth and set my napkin on my empty plate. "What else is on your agenda today? Do you need to run a hundred miles? Are you going to climb Mount Everest on your lunch break?"

"Nah. I'll save that for next week." Finn stands and takes our plates to the sink. "I'm watching the DC Stars hockey game later."

"DC? Not a fan of the Chicago team?"

"They're not bad, but Maverick Miller is unstoppable and damn fun to watch. Before that, I have some work I need to do."

"Work?" I frown. "Are you stitching people up in your home office?"

"Not exactly." He rubs his jaw, and it's obvious he's weighing something in his mind. "Do you want to see?"

"Oh, fuck no. This is the part where you murder me, isn't it? Katarina has my location, so she'll know exactly where to send the police." I stand and hold my fork out in front of me. "Come any closer, and I'll jab your eyes out."

"You're cute." He stands too, and I have to crane my neck to hold his gaze. "It's good your friend knows where you are when you're hanging out with a stranger, but I'm not going to murder you."

"That's exactly what a murderer would say."

His eyes twinkle with amusement, and he chuckles. "Pretty sure a murderer would have offed you in your sleep. It's a lot less work than going up against a fork."

"See? Your brain is working like a serial killer's."

"Do you want to tie my hands behind my back?" Finn holds up his wrists. "You can. Might turn me on, but at least you'd feel safer."

I consider him and slowly lower the fork to my side. "You can show me, but one wrong move, and I'm going to stab you."

"Now I'm even more turned on." He hooks his thumb over his shoulder and winks. "Come on. I'll show you my torture chamber."

ELEVEN

FINN

WHEN WE STOP outside my home office, I turn and face her. She smirks and holds the utensil under my chin, and I want to kiss her until she's begging me to let her come.

"Is this your lair?" she asks, and I nod.

"It is. I don't make it a habit to lie, but there's something else I wasn't honest with you about." I run my hand through my hair, knowing I'm going to look like a jackass once I open the door. "You were right the other day about me sounding like the guy who narrated the romance book you were listening to. It probably was me. It's something I do on the side. Not many people know about it, and it caught me off guard when you said you recognized my voice."

"I *knew* it." Margo pokes my side with the fork. "When you whispered I was a good girl last night, I swear I was having déjà vu."

"I'm sorry. I don't want you to think I'm hiding shit from you. I'm not. It's just…" I shrug and put my hands in my pockets. "Some people might not consider it a career, but it's damn hard work."

"I don't doubt it. How do you get into something like that?"

"It's a long story that involves a different TikTok video a coworker posted of me."

"So, what you're saying is you are internet famous? Got it."

"I guess, and that's alarming. I enjoy the gig, but I'm behind schedule on a project I've been working on. I should've been recording last night, but I got distracted."

My eyes drop to the hickey I left on her neck. Her skin is already turning a faint purple, and I reach forward and rub my thumb over the mark. Margo sighs and tilts her head to the side, the fork falling from her grasp.

"What were you distracted by?" she murmurs, teasing me when she pulls the hem of the shirt up her thighs so I can see she's not wearing any underwear. I groan when she drops the cotton and covers herself back up. "Must've been important."

"Very important." I cup her cheek, and the urge to touch her pulses through me. I might've had my fill of her last night, but now that it's morning, I need her again. I need her over and over again, so I walk her backward until her shoulders press against the wall. I rest my hands next to her head, caging her in, and drop my mouth to her throat. "I know you're stuck here until the roads clear, but do you mind if I do some work this morning?"

Her breathing hitches, and she rests a warm palm on the center of my chest. Her fingers drag down my skin with sharp nails, and my hips buck forward at the contact. "Can I listen?" she whispers. "I promise I'll be quiet."

"It's really not that exciting."

"Maybe not, but I've always wondered how the narrators get into character. Do you read the book beforehand to get a feel for the person you're voicing?"

"Some narrators rely on the information sheet the author provides us about the characters and their personalities." I tuck a piece of her wild hair behind her ear and sink my teeth gently into her neck. "I prefer to read the book. Helps me get in the right headspace and understand the person I'm voicing."

"That's so cool."

"It pays the bills. You really want to listen?"

"I do." She nods eagerly. "And I promise I won't make fun of your reading voice. I had your tongue inside me last night, so I'm not one to judge what noises you might make."

"If you behave, maybe you can have my tongue inside you again when I finish." Her cheeks flush a pretty shade of pink, and I lower my mouth to hers. I kiss her, wanting to taste her again after going without her for too many hours. "Can you do that, Margo?"

"Yeah." Margo swallows and drops her hand between us, cupping my half-hard dick. I blow out a shaky breath when she strokes her fingers up and down my length. "Can *you*, Finn?"

"Yes," I say, but I forget what we're talking about because she snaps the waistband of my sweatpants on my skin, and I moan.

"Good boy," she murmurs, and I almost come on the spot.

"You are a fucking minx."

"You like it."

I do like it.

Probably more than I should, because the second the plows come through and clear the streets, she's out of here and we'll be over.

I better make the last few hours we have together damn fun. I don't want her to forget about me.

"Ready to see where I hide all the bodies?" I ask, and she laughs.

"Hack me up, Finn."

I step away from her because if I stand any closer, I'll fuck her against the wall. It's something I've been thinking about since last night, but with this deadline looming, I need to focus.

Work first.

Then I can have her.

I turn the knob and nudge the door open with my hip. I hold her hand as we walk inside, and she looks around the room.

I converted the space into a soundproof office so I don't have to rent a studio or carry my equipment with me anywhere. It's been fine up to this point, but I'd like something nicer one day, with a little more space and better technology.

"Well?" I ask.

"This is so cool. You have so much gear." She drags her finger down the body of the shotgun microphone on my desk. "Do you use it all?"

"Depends on what I'm recording, but most of the time, yeah. You've listened to audiobooks before; you know any sort of outside noise within the narration can be a distraction."

"Oh my god. I was listening to a book where I could hear a clock ticking in the background. I thought I was going to lose my mind."

"See? That's exactly what I'm talking about."

I walk to my desk and grab my script, flipping to the spot I left off the a few days ago. Turning on my mic, I watch Margo settle into the chair across from me, her eyes wide.

"What book is it?" she asks.

"A stalker romance. The scene I'm doing involves him watching her get off while he's hiding in the closet. She doesn't know he's there."

"That's hot."

"Kinky, huh? Kind of pushes the line of consent, but I tell myself it's fiction." I clear my throat and hold up my lines. "The mic picks up tons of feedback, so I need you to be as quiet as you can."

"Someone is demanding." Margo pouts but follows it up with a smile. "I can be quiet."

"Good girl," I say, and she lights up like she did last night when I held her hands above her head in my bed. When I told her to get on her knees and get me off only using her mouth.

I slip on my headphones, hit record, and start reading from the beginning of the chapter, losing myself in the words and the storytelling.

It's one of the darker books I've narrated, but the morally gray character is charming. Funny, even, and a nice guy. You can't help but root for him, and I channel that enthusiasm into each syllable and every word. I hold my pauses and draw out the questions of his inner monologue, wanting the listeners to think they're actually in his head.

When I get to the part where he's watching the female main character, Maxine, but not touching, I look up and see Margo with her mouth half parted. Her cheeks are red and her chest is heaving. Her eyes lock on mine and she blinks, sitting back in the chair like she's been caught doing something very, very bad.

I pause my recording and smile. "You're distracting me."

"I am? Shit. I'm sorry."

"Are you doing okay over there?"

"Yeah. No." She crosses her legs then uncrosses them. "It's just… hot. Really hot."

"What is?"

"You reading the things she's doing to herself. Your voice. Picturing it and imagining it was me." Margo flushes an even darker shade of red. "I'm sorry. I can keep my mouth shut."

I take off my headphones and stand, walking around the desk and sitting on the edge. I don't want her to think I'm mad at her, so I lean forward and rub the top of her knee, humming when her legs part and I can see how wet she is.

She's fucking soaked and practically staining the leather chair. I groan, wanting nothing more than to say *fuck work* and go down on her right now.

"Look how turned on you are." I drag my thumb through her pussy, and she arches her back. "You're so needy, aren't you, Margo? Distracting me while I'm trying to work. Getting turned on. Wishing you had a bad man with a mask hiding in your closet."

"I'll go in the other room." She's panting, and I smirk. One night with her, and I can read her like a book. She's enjoying this. She wants *more* of this, and I'm always aim to please. I'm not letting her go anywhere. "I didn't mean to get in your way."

"Get naked," I tell her. "And sit back in the chair. Whatever I read from the script, I want you to do to yourself. We'll call it research."

"Won't the mic pick up on the noises?"

"It will, so you better be quiet unless you want thousands of readers to hear how wet you get from letting your ex-boyfriend's dad watch you get off."

Margo swallows. I don't expect her to actually do it, and I don't care if she says no. It won't make me want her any less; if anything, it'll make me want to hurry the fuck up and finish recording so I can drag her back to my bedroom.

She surprises me when she rips off her shirt and tosses it on the floor. She scoots back and hooks her legs over the arms of the chair, wide open and so fucking ready for me.

God.

She might be my dream woman.

"Keep reading, Mr. Mathieson," she says.

It's almost impossible to move back to my desk, but I walk around the piece of furniture and pick up where I left off, tempted to jerk off while I read out loud.

"*Her back arches off the bed as she plays with her clit,*" I read, and my eyes bounce from the script to Margo. Her fingers touch herself and she bites down on her lower lip, trying her best to muffle her sounds. "*I study the circles she's using. She likes to draw it out as long as possible. She likes to tease herself. Maxine is quiet at first, but a moan sneaks out of her, and I shove my hand down my pants to stop myself from making the same noise.*"

Another glance at Margo tells me she's mimicking the chapter exactly as I'm reading it. She drops her head back and rubs her clit slowly with two fingers, and I have to adjust myself again.

"*I could watch her for hours,*" I continue. "*Especially when she pinches her nipples and then fumbles in her bedside drawer for the pink vibrator I know she bought yesterday.*"

Margo tips her head up and looks around frantically. I hit pause on the recording and pull my phone from my pocket, tossing it to her.

"What is this for?" she asks.

"Swipe to the third page. There's a vibrator app. Hold it against your clit."

"You have a *vibrator app*? That is not normal."

"The last woman I hooked up with loved toys. I downloaded it so I could set it on her lap when we were out in public and watch her get off."

Margo stares at me, and I think I see a touch of jealousy in her gaze. Her green eyes narrow for the briefest of seconds, and I debate telling her about the times I've been jealous of my goddamn son, knowing he got to be the one to touch her.

He stopped by my place after seeing her one afternoon, and he smelled like sex. Like he had spent hours in bed with her, and now I know he was probably selfish. He probably only got himself off without taking care of *her* needs, and that makes a flicker of rage start at the base of my spine.

I'm going to let her get off right now, then I'm going to get her off again with my cock, knowing I'm one of only a few who know how to take care of her. Smugness rolls through me when her lips curl into a grin, egging me on.

"Okay." She taps on the phone screen with her free hand and rests it on top of her pussy. "*Fuck.* That feels good."

"Keep doing what I tell you to do, Margo," I say, turning my attention back to the script. "*Maxine holds the vibrator against her clit, changing the speed so it pulses against her. Her moans echo in the room, and I swear to fucking god I hear her say my name before she pushes the toy inside her cunt, filling herself and spreading her legs open so I get the perfect view of her stuffed pussy.*"

Margo trembles and glances down at my phone. "I can't fuck myself with this."

I turn off the mic again. I'm going to have to spend a shit ton of time editing, but I don't care. It's worth it to see her like this; horny. On the brink of an orgasm. Her hair a mess and her eyes heated with desire.

"The Christmas ornament." I point at the ceramic tree

on the corner of my desk, and she bursts out laughing. "Fuck yourself with that."

"Oh, fuck no. You're a goddamn paramedic, Finn. You've seen those viral videos of doctors warning you *not* to shove foreign objects inside yourself, right? I'm not going to the emergency room because I have a holiday decoration lodged in my vagina."

That makes me laugh too. "I made one of those videos last year for the hospital." I open the desk drawer and pull out a condom, tossing it her way. "Put this on so it's clean, and only insert the top of the ornament. Do not go past the first layer of branches, or you'll hurt yourself."

Margo looks at me like I'm insane, and I know there's no way in *hell* she's actually going to go through with this.

Nobody would.

She sets the phone on her chest. She leans forward and grabs the ornament. I watch with wonder as she opens the condom wrapper and slowly covers the ceramic with the latex, and I almost fall out of my chair because I'm so goddamn surprised.

TWELVE
MARGO

I'M GOING TO HELL.

There's no way I make it through the pearly gates now, not when I'm down here about to fuck myself with a Christmas ornament while a man I barely know watches me.

Jesus is probably rolling in his grave because of what a ho-ho-hoe I am.

I've officially lost my mind, but as I spit on the tip of the condom-covered ornament and slowly push it inside myself, I don't give a damn about being sane.

"*Fuck*," I moan.

The ornament is thicker than any toy I've used. It takes a few seconds of adjusting, but soon I welcome the unusual sensation as my sore thighs open wider to accommodate the new stretch.

"Not too deep," Finn warns, and his voice is closer than it was before. I open my eyes and find him standing, his hand on the desk and his attention on me. "Just a little more, Margo, then you need to stop."

For as enjoyable as this ornament is, I want his cock

instead. I want him buried inside me like he was last night, and I miss his body on mine.

I press the Christmas tree another inch forward and groan, feeling so good while doing something wrong.

"Put the phone back on your clit while I finish recording," he says, and I love how commanding his voice is. It snaps me into action, and I move the phone low on my stomach as the vibrations ripple through me.

"It's too much." I squeeze my eyes shut, overstimulated. "Why aren't you fucking me?"

"Be a good girl and be patient, Margo." He clears his throat and starts reading again. "*Maxine is making the same noises she made when I heard her come last week, and I can tell she's close. She twists her wrist to find a new angle and lifts her back off the bed. Her feet drag up the sheets and her toes curl. I wonder what she would look like on the back of my motorcycle. What she would look like riding the handle of a knife or the barrel of a gun. Unbelievable, I bet. She fucks herself harder, and I watch, mesmerized, when she cries out. She moans so loud, I'm sure her neighbors can hear, and I give into temptation, stroking myself as she comes on the toy I wish was my cock.*"

My own moan matches the one the girl in the book might be making. This is mind-blowing. The filthiest and most depraved thing I've ever done, but I don't care, because the orgasm is so good, so *new*, I fall apart piece by piece.

I don't have time to come down from the high because the improvised toy is pulled out of me. Warm hands rest on my thigh and a thumb presses on my clit. I buck my hips, searching for the friction I just had, and when I open my eyes, Finn is stroking his cock.

"Fuck me," I whisper. "Hard. Rough."

"I still have the recording going."

"Don't care." I tug on his sweatpants until they fall to the ground. "Let everyone hear."

"I knew I liked you." Finn laughs when I reach for him, and he laces our fingers together. "Was what we did last night okay, Margo? Did you like all of that? Do you want me to try something different?"

I've spent less than twenty-four hours with him, but it feels like I *know* him. Like this kindness isn't an act he's putting on to get some action. He truly means it, and I rest a hand on his cheek.

"Last night was perfect." I sink my teeth into his lower lip, happy to hear his soft grunt when I smooth over the bite with the tip of my tongue. "It's your last chance, Finn. Make me remember you."

That fuels the fire in him, because he's putting a condom on his cock. Lining up with my entrance and gripping my thighs with that strength I like about him. When our eyes meet, I give him a small nod, and he turns his cheek to kiss the inside of my palm.

He pushes the head of his cock inside my pussy, and I groan. "We both know you're not going to forget me anytime soon."

He's so damn right, and I hate him because of it.

Without any of last night's fanfare, without any of the foreplay we did the first and second and third times we were together, he buries himself in me, sinking all the way in until I can feel him *everywhere*.

"God," I grit out. He's the longest and thickest I've ever had, and talking is difficult. "You're so good at this."

"Your nicknames are cute. Finn is just fine." He braces his hands on the curve of the chair behind me and rolls his hips. "I've been fucking women for years, and no one's felt as good as you."

I'm almost folded like a pretzel, but his words are charming.

I know it's a line he's using to make the moment more intimate and personal. He doesn't actually believe it, but for half a second, I pretend like he does.

I pretend like this is something we do every day, and it's the only reason why I run my palms across his shoulders and whisper, "Kiss me, Finn."

His lips capture mine, and I put everything I have into our kiss. It makes up for the shit I endured with Jeremy. For my years of crappy dating and this deep-rooted fear I have about never wanting to settle down because I might not be good enough.

It's like we're playing a game to see who's the most aggressive, and I think Finn might be winning because he cups my cheek. He drives into me at the same time his tongue brushes against mine, and I never thought rough sex could also be so sweet and sensual.

From this angle, he can get deeper than he did last night. He uses his height to his advantage as he thrusts forward, our bodies connecting and finding a rhythm I've never experienced with another partner.

The slap of our skin echoes around us, but my moans drown it out. His fingers move to my hips, holding me as the sharp bite of his nails leave half-moon marks on the curves of my body.

"Fucking love your cunt," Finn says breathlessly. He stares down at me, a laser-sharp focus on my tits as they bounce. "How can I make this better for you, Margo?"

"Could you..." I trail off and take his left hand, guiding it up my stomach. He pinches my nipples, and I suck in a sharp breath, dragging his touch higher. "My throat. I want you to squeeze my throat."

His eyes flare with lust. "Yeah?"

"Yeah." I nod and his fingers curl around my neck. "Tighter."

"If it's too much, you tap my thigh, understand?"

"Yes, Daddy," I joke, and I don't miss the way he slams into me extra hard. How his thumb strokes up and down my windpipe as pleasure builds low in my belly. "That feels so good."

We match each other's enthusiasm, a push and pull that has me lifting my hips to meet his thrusts and his grip on my neck tightening ever so slightly. Our panting is synchronized, and when Finn squeezes *just* hard enough to turn the edges of my vision blurry, I know I'm close to falling apart.

"I'm close," I whisper. My energy is waning and I can feel the twelve hours of aggressive fucking catching up to me. "And once I finish, I want you to fill me up."

"Goddamn." He folds his body over mine. His thighs knock against the edge of the chair and the hand at my throat moves to my head. He pulls on the ends of my hair hard enough for my neck to jerk back and look at him. "I could worship your pussy all day. Come for me, Margo. Show me how well you can milk my cock."

That deep voice does me in and I cry out, the orgasm crashing into me like a wave. It wraps me up tight, a full-body experience I feel all the way down to my toes. I convulse and shake, riding the high for longer than I ever have in my life.

Finn's movements turn sloppy. His words come out slurred and his eyes roll to the back of his head when I use my remaining energy to hold my legs open so his cock can reach new places. With another quick slap of his hips, he groans. His release sneaks up on him when I touch his ass and run my finger over the curve of his backside.

"*Hell*," he gasps, and he stills inside me. "I've never done that before."

"You don't think this is heaven?" I wince when he pulls out of me, my legs sore and heavy. "And it might be time to admit you're an ass man, Mr. Mathieson."

He carefully rolls the condom down his length and ties it off, tossing it in the trash can in the corner of the room. Finn grabs the forgotten ornament sitting on his desk and drops to his knees, his mouth pressing hot kisses to the inside of my thigh.

"Can you give me one more?" he asks, brushing the top of the Christmas tree along my entrance. He licks my clit, and I whine. "One more before you hit the road."

I'm not sure if I have it in me, but all fears about my lack of energy evaporate when Finn worships me, coaxing me to a third orgasm as he gently talks me through the rush of adrenaline flooding my veins. It's quick and sharp, surprising me when he spits on my pussy then rubs the saliva over the ornament. The bliss of the last twenty minutes settles in my bones, and tears prick behind my eyes.

"I can't—" I beg.

It's too much.

I'm too tired. Too exhausted to do anything else.

Finn drops the ornament to the ground, and it shatters to pieces. He scoops me in his arms and changes our positions, sitting in the chair and cradling me in his arms.

"I've got you," he whispers, stroking my hair. "You're okay."

Bone-deep exhaustion racks my body, and a sob sneaks out of me. "I'm sorry. I don't know why—"

"Lots of stimulation. Not enough sleep. It's my fault. I should've—"

"You've been perfect," I blurt, because he has been.

My one-night stands have never been so mindful or satisfying, and I want him to know that. "I just need a minute."

"Take all the minutes you need." Finn kisses my forehead and peels my sweat-soaked hair away from my skin. "I'm here when you're ready."

"You're pretty great, you know." I close my eyes and snuggle into him, the hint of that peppermint I tasted last night lingering this morning. "Thank you."

"Thank *you*." His fingers dance down my spine and I sigh, content and worn out. "Wish I could wrap you up with a bow and put you under my tree."

"Maybe we'll run into each other next year at a different bar."

"Maybe we will." He stands and walks us to the door. "Ready for a bath?"

"You spoil me." My eyes flutter closed, and I'm half asleep as he heads down the hall. "A very, very nice guy."

His laugh is warm and rich. It's a sound I'd like to commit to memory to remember how good this entire experience has been. "'Tis the season for nice guys, Margo Andrews."

THIRTEEN

MARGO

"I'M HERE." I kick off my shoes in Katarina's foyer and head down the hall in my socks. "Sorry I'm late."

"Are you sorry?" Katarina asks when I walk into her kitchen. "Or did you have a good time with the hot paramedic?"

I give her a sly grin. "You looked at my location, didn't you?"

"Of course I looked at your location. You didn't answer my texts, and I wanted to make sure you were alive."

"My little creep. That's why I love you: you'd storm into a stranger's apartment if I disappeared for more than twenty-four hours."

"Mhm." She points to the barstool at the island. "Sit and spill. You were with him all night?"

"And today." I sit and relax on the cushioned leather. I'm so tired and sore. Everything hurts and I desperately want to curl up in bed, but I told Kat I'd be here for dinner tonight, and I don't want to skip out on our plans. "We left the bar after you all did, but not before he told me he's Jeremy's dad."

"*What*?" Kat cracks open a bottle of wine and lifts it in my direction. I nod, and she pours two servings. "Are you serious?"

"Yup. That didn't stop me from sleeping with him, though, so I'm not sure what it says about me. Probably that I have daddy issues." I laugh and knock my glass against hers. "He's a good guy. He even cooked me breakfast this morning. But the best part? He made me laugh, and we had fun."

"You need to back up. You didn't realize who he was before we sat with them at the bar?"

"Nope. I haven't met him. I think I saw him in passing once, but nothing long enough that would've given me any indication of who he was. Finding out he's my ex's dad didn't bother me as much as I thought it would."

"Holy shit, Margo. How was it?" Kat asks, sitting beside me. "Give me all the details."

"It was…" I bite my lower lip and hold back a smile.

There are too many adjectives I want to use, and it's silly to admit how fluttery my heart has been since last night.

I'm not sure how to describe it all, if we're being honest.

Nice is too much of an understatement and *out of this world* feels more on point.

It was horny and hot and by far the kinkiest encounter I've ever had with a man, but there was something deep, something special buried under the sexual component.

Finn and I really got to know each other. Over breakfast. When he put me in the tub and washed my hair, telling me what it was like being a solo parent. After, when he dried me off and warmed me up back in his bed, showing off photos of all the cool places he's run and how lucky he feels to go out and breathe fresh air every morning.

It was like I'd known him for years.

I thought our goodbye would be awkward, some weird song and dance we did around each other as I put on my skirt and boots and he handed me my beanie, but it wasn't. He pulled me into a hug and kissed the top of my head, thanking me for a night he won't forget.

I'm sure as hell not going to forget it either.

I can still feel his fingers running up my thigh. The heat of his mouth on my neck and the sound of his laughter ringing in my ear. He's imprinted himself on me, and the tiniest part of me wishes I could wind the clock back and forget him. Wishes I'd never met him, because I don't know how the hell I'm supposed to move on from something that was never mine to have.

I could've broken the rules and asked for his number, but we did exactly what we decided we would do. As soon as the streets cleared and the plows came through, I climbed into an Uber and gave him a salute, caught off guard when I glanced out the window and found him watching my car drive away, his hands shoved in his pocket and the twist of a frown on his mouth.

Everything happens for a reason, and I'm beginning to wonder if Finn was the universe's gift to me. A clean slate and a friendly reminder of all the good things in the world with his kind heart and gentle soul.

And his filthy fucking mouth.

I shiver and know my vibrator is going to be a sad substitute for his fingers and cock.

"Wonderful," I finally land on. "It was wonderful. He was wonderful. If we weren't at different places in our lives, maybe it could've been something."

"Why can't it be something?" Kat takes a sip of wine and assesses me. "You're not eighteen, Margo. You have your shit figured out, and you're more mature than a lot of other women in the world."

"I am, but I'm only twenty-four. He's forty. That's almost a lifetime older than me, and I just got out of a shitty relationship. I don't think the best idea is to dive into another one with the guy's *dad*."

"See? You're self-aware, which is a very mature thing to be."

I laugh. "It was sex, Kat. I don't need to romanticize every interaction I have with a man and make it a bigger deal than it really is. Finn and I fucked. We had a good time together, and that's it. End of story."

"Out of all the guys you've been with, where does he rank?"

"Top of the list," I say with no hesitation. "He makes everyone else seem like… *boys*."

"I'm so damn jealous. I had to listen to his friend talk about fifteen different kinds of plant species." When I give her a weird look, she snorts. "He has a green thumb. His living room is covered in plants, apparently, and I got a lesson on which time of year produces the best sunlight for various growing patterns. The drive was eight minutes, Margo. My brain was going to explode."

"Wow." I rest my chin on the palm of my hand and smile. "You know a lot about the guy you spent half a second with."

"He was fine. He walked me to the door of the building and waited in the cold until I was upstairs." She waves me off. "But we're not talking about me. We're talking about you. Does Finn live alone?"

"Yup. In a nice brownstone not far from here. I'd been there a few times with Jeremy, but obviously didn't make the connection. He's financially independent. Friendly with Jeremy's mom, but not in love with her. An athlete who's a damn fast runner, and an overall good guy."

"You are *blushing*." Kat pinches my cheek, and I laugh again. "You had a lot of fun with him, didn't you?"

"I did. And I mean besides the sex. One-night stands are supposed to be awkward, you know? There's always that uncomfortable moment where you have to politely tell them to put on their clothes without seeming like a bitch. And on the flip side, if you ask them to hang around, you'll come off as needy and go against everything you agreed on. This was very… adult. We weren't fumbling around or making small talk neither of us cared about."

"And you don't want to see him again," she says.

"It's not that I don't want to see him. I just don't think there's anything there. Sure, there's a physical attraction, but the dude works in a hospital. He doesn't want to hear about the homework I give my kids or when the next Scholastic Book Fair is."

"Fuck." Katarina sighs. "I loved the Book Fair."

"Why do you think I'm a teacher? That was the high-light of my childhood." I swirl my drink and shrug. "I appreciated the time Finn and I had together, but it's in the past now, and that's okay."

"Well, you have my support if you decide to bang him again." She reaches for me and squeezes my hand. "And that hickey you have on your neck is gnarly, my friend."

I touch the warm skin and shake my head. "He was… possessive. But a *good* possessive. I might have egged him on a little by asking if he would know how to take care of me, and I'm happy to report he did."

"That's my girl. Gosh, it's good to see you happy. We both know Jeremy wasn't a forever thing, but you haven't smiled like this… ever, I don't think."

She's probably right, and she's known me since I moved to the city four years ago. We met on Bumble BFF, both looking for someone who liked to eat copious amounts of food and sit on the couch with a good book.

It's funny; I came to Chicago for a job, but I ended up finding my best friend.

I can't imagine my life without Kat in it, and I thank my lucky stars every day I decided to meet up with her at a neighborhood farmers' market. Without her, I'd be lost and sad, and life is too short to be either of those things.

"Maybe the Christmas cheer is rubbing off on me," I tease, finishing off my wine. "I was promised chocolate chip cookies, but I'm sitting here empty-handed. Something is wrong with this picture."

Kat bops my nose and jumps up, kissing my cheek. "Don't underestimate how much the Christmas gods of fate want things to go their way."

I grin and join her at the counter to roll out the dough, holding back the urge to tell her I kind of hope seeing Finn again is how things are supposed to go.

FOURTEEN

FINN

"HOW ARE WE FEELING THIS MORNING?" Rhett asks at the starting line of the Dashing All The Way 5k. "You disappeared the last few days. Thought you might be sick or something."

"Nah. I was busy with work." I lift my leg and rotate my knee out to stretch my groin. "Did you miss me?"

I haven't told them about Margo.

It's been three days since I put her in an Uber and watched her drive away, and she's still on my mind.

I know they wouldn't make fun of me for thinking about her; if my buddies didn't tease me about hooking up with a woman who purposely peed the bed so she could record how guys reacted, I doubt they'll give me shit for having a fun night with someone that involved zero urination. (And yes, that's a true story.)

I don't understand *why* I can't shake the thought of Margo, though. I've had one-night stands before. I've had a quick hookup in a hotel bar with a stranger whose name I didn't learn. Hell, I've had serious girlfriends, with some of the relationships lasting a year.

So why the fuck is this girl driving me crazy?

Maybe it was her laugh or the way she batted her eyelashes. It might be the confidence she has, not an ounce of shyness to her game. Honestly, it's probably her smile and the way her eyes twinkle when she's happy that's pulling me in.

Whatever it is, I need it to *stop*.

"In your dreams," Rhett says, and it's a yank back to reality. He takes a sip of his water and tosses it in the trash can on the other side of the barricade. "What are you going for this morning? A PR? Running for a certain time?"

"I feel pretty good." I shake out my arms and pull my sunglasses over my eyes. "Beautiful day for a race. Might fuck around and shoot for a personal record."

"Beautiful day? It's freezing." Holden tugs on his gloves and shivers. "Running in weather below thirty-five degrees should be illegal."

"You grew up in Illinois. How do you still think this is cold?" I ask.

"Because I'm a sensitive man who prefers the warmer climate."

"Run faster so you can finish sooner." I pat his shoulder and nod hello to the row of guys up front. This race always attracts the college boys who are home for the holidays, and I like lining up next to them. They think I'm some old guy who can't throw down negative splits, and it's fun to see the surprise on their faces when I pass them in the last mile. "And stop complaining."

"We're doing lunch after this, right?" Rhett asks. "I told Jada we could go to that new pasta restaurant up the street from our house."

"Sounds good to me. Last one in has to buy for everyone."

"Not fair," Holden groans. "You all know I'm the slowest of the three of us."

"You're not slow, H. You run at your own pace," I tell him. "And what do I always say?"

"Miles are miles no matter how fast," he grumbles, and I nod.

"Exactly right, my friend." I click my watch and hover my finger over the start button. "I'll see you kids on the other side."

The race announcer blows an air horn and I take off, dodging a six-year-old who's about to get mowed over by a pack of very ambitious runners.

I exhale a breath as my lungs adjust to the bite of cold nipping at my nose. Holden might complain about it being freezing, but you can't dream up a better morning to go for a run. The air is still. The sky is clear, and the sun makes everything feel infinitely warmer.

At the half mile mark, I settle into my pace, knowing my competition likes to go out too fast before they start to drop like flies. I prefer the longer distances over the shorter sprint stuff, but it's fun to change it up once in a while.

Like today.

I'm cruising well below my 5k PR pace of fourteen minutes, a time I haven't hit since my early twenties. The effort feels easy as I enjoy the moment and keep an eye on the leader out in front. A kid with a sign cheers me on, and I give a halfhearted wave to the volunteers blocking traffic for us.

The pain starts at halfway.

The familiar burn in my legs works its way up from my calves to my quads. My hamstrings scream at me when I climb a small incline, and I curse under my breath at whoever the fuck decided on this course.

When I cross the two-mile mark four seconds ahead of

my PR, I know I have to make a decision; I either need to go for it now, or I'm going to run out of ground. I don't have twenty more miles to chip away at the guy ahead of me.

Fuck it.

Might as well make my last race of the year a fun one.

Gritting my teeth, I round a bend and search for the well inside me I tap into when I need to dig deep. When I need to grind a little harder to accomplish my goals, and I pass fifth place, then fourth.

My body feels like it's revolting against me.

I never thought I'd be wishing I was running five times this distance.

My legs are heavy like lead and my lungs sting with the mid-December cold.

Everything *hurts*, but when I pass third place, I wipe the snot from my nose and put my head down, ready to finish this damn thing.

I hang behind the guy in second place for thirty seconds, matching his stride as I kick it up a notch.

Margo's face appears in my blurry vision. I picture her teasing me for being so fast, the look of admiration in her eyes when I told her how many marathons I've done. It makes me smile, and as a knife of pain wedges itself in my lower back, I veer around second place until there's only one guy left to take down.

I recognize him from the singlet he's wearing. He's in a different run club in the city, and I've never really liked him. He's showboaty when he wins, the kind of athlete who posts on social media like he's god's gift to the sport.

It's fun to be fast, but it's really fucking lame to make other people feel like they're inadequate just because they don't run the pace you do.

With a quarter mile to go, I surge forward. My feet

pound the pavement and I cross three miles, thirty seconds away from wrapping this up with a nice decorative bow. I pass him, our shoulders brushing as the race announcer calls out our names to the cheer of a crowd.

Eight-tenths of a mile turns to seven-tenths, then six. I pick up my cadence. My feet turn over as fast as they will go, and I'm the one to break the tape at the finish. I lift my arms over my head in celebration and slow to a jog, leaving everything I had in me out on the course.

"Shit." I lean over the metal barricade and swallow down the bile rising in my throat. I shrug off the medic who comes over to look at me and stand up straight. "I'm fine. Just need to walk it off."

I put my hands over my head and shuffle past the finish line. My breathing finally returns to normal and my heart rate slows to its resting pace.

When the possibility of projectile vomit subsides, I loop around on the outside of the course so I can watch the rest of the runners come in.

Men make up the first fifteen finishers, but I spot a familiar blonde charging toward the finish as the first female. I laugh when she crosses the line, waving her down after she lifts her head up from between her knees.

"Katarina," I call out, and she blinks at me with the dazed look runners get when they've pushed themselves past the point of exhaustion. I grab a bottle of water and meet her at the barricade, handing over the hydration. "Damn, you're fast."

"Thanks." She holds the water bottle to her forehead and exhales a shaky breath. "Been training for this one. Didn't realize I was in the lead."

"Incredible run. College cross country?"

"Yup. D1. Finished third at the national championships."

"Impressive." I scan the finish line, not sure why I think I'd find Margo in the seventeen-minute group. I doubt she's here, unless it was to support her friend, but I look for her anyway. "Nice job out there."

"She'll be here in a bit." Katarina props her foot up on the curb to stretch her calf and groans. "Margo. Right around thirty minutes."

I perk up. "She's here?"

"Yeah. She almost backed out this morning, but I think she was excited to try again and not end up in a medical tent this time."

I laugh. "That would be much preferred. Do you know what she's wearing?"

"A shirt that says *tequila made me do it.*"

"Do you think—" I lick my lips and clear my throat. "Would she mind if I was waiting for her at the finish line?"

"I think she'd like that very much." Katarina eyes me and gives me a smile. "I don't get weird vibes from you, and she was very happy when she got back from your place. You did something right."

I don't know why that makes me giddy, but it's enough confirmation for me to stick around. I give her shoulder a light squeeze and head to the end of the finish line chute. "Thanks for the reassurance."

Rhett comes in a few minutes later, and Holden is behind him. I watch the waves of finishers cross the line and search for her. The time on the clock tells me she's probably still five minutes away, but a flash of color heading into the last one tenth of a mile catches my attention, and I hightail it to the volunteers handing out medals.

"Hi," I say to one of the women. "Do you mind if I give one of the participants a medal? It's her first 5k, and I want to surprise her."

"Oh, of course." The woman hands me a medal and a mylar blanket. "Are you proposing to her too?"

"What?" I burst out laughing and shake my head. "No ma'am. We've only hung out once."

"Sometimes that's all it takes to know." She winks and turns to congratulate a mother pushing a stroller.

"And coming across the line is Margo Andrews from Chicago. Give it up for Margo, everyone," the announcer says to the crowd, and I move forward so she doesn't miss me.

A quick assessment shows me she's in better shape than after the half marathon, and I breathe a sigh of relief.

"Hey," I say, and her eyes snap up to meet mine. "I've said it once, but I'll say it again. We have *got* to stop meeting like this."

FIFTEEN
MARGO

FINN IS HERE.

In front of me.

Shirtless, sweaty, and holding out a medal.

I blink and stare at him, wondering what the hell is going on.

"You ran?" I ask, which feels like the dumbest thing in the world to say.

Obviously he ran.

There's a bib attached to his shorts and a medal around his neck. His cheeks are red and there is dried sweat along his hairline. I want to kick myself for how silly I sound.

"I did. And so did you." He holds out the medal and I dip my head so he can put it on me. "Congratulations on your first 5k. How do you feel?"

"Marginally better than the half marathon, but also like I want to puke. Is that normal?"

"Totally normal. Let's get you some water and Gatorade."

"This feels familiar."

"There's less collapsing this time, so we're off to a better start." He offers me his arm and I rest my hand on his biceps to balance. "What was your time?"

I check my watch. "Twenty-eight minutes and forty-five seconds."

"Damn, Miss Andrews. That's impressive work, my friend."

It's funny to hear him call me his friend after the filthy things he said the other night. After he easily tossed around names like *baby*, but I like the way it rolls off his tongue. I like imagining a world where we can be cordial with each other, even after sleeping together.

"It is?" I ask.

"It certainly is. You should be proud of yourself."

His praise lights me up, and I'm warmer than I was when I was exerting myself on the course. Nothing about it is condescending, and it makes me feel like I accomplished something important. Like I did a good job, and I never thought I'd be so proud of a physical achievement.

"Thanks," I say, and a weird burst of emotion sits in the middle of my chest. I accept a sports drink from a volunteer and twist open the cap. "What was your time?"

"Fourteen minutes and some change."

"Holy shit." I choke on my sip of yellow Gatorade and wipe my mouth with the back of my hand. "You are unreal."

"It was a good day. I saw Katarina, by the way. She was the first female, and she told me you'd be here. I, uh, hope it's okay I'm accosting you at the finish line." Finn pushes his sunglasses up his nose and looks away. "If you want to get rid of me, I'll leave you be."

"No." I grip his arm tighter, pulled to him like a magnet. "I like having you greet me after I've returned from the depths of hell."

His laugh is light, and he leads us to the field where runners and spectators are reuniting. "It sucks, doesn't it?"

"I'm never doing another one."

"Yeah. I said that too. Now look at me." He lifts his arm and waves to the two guys we sat with the other night at the bar. I spot Katarina with them, and a brunette woman I don't recognize. "Want to come say hi to my friends?"

"As long as I'm not interrupting the club of fast athletes or anything. I'd hate to bring down the average pace of the group by five minutes."

"Stop that." He touches my hip, and I shiver at the contact. I've missed the feel of his palm on my body. How he dragged his fingers across my chest and down my stomach. I got off to the thought of him last night, imagining he was watching me from his desk while I fucked myself with a toy instead of a Christmas ornament. My cheeks burn at the memory, and I wonder if he can read minds, because his mouth curls up in one of his devastating smirks. "What did I tell you about self-deprecation?"

"To not do it."

"Exactly. And you're not interrupting anything."

"Okay." I tug on my shirt, wishing I had brought a change of clothes. "If you say so."

"I definitely say so. What are you doing after this? Do you have any plans?"

"Am I supposed to do something other than sit on my couch the rest of the afternoon and wallow in pain?"

"Nope. That sounds like the perfect day." He laughs again and plays with the end of my ponytail. "Come back to my place," he murmurs, dropping his voice low. "You can shower, and I'll stretch you out."

"There's no way in hell I can bend the ways I did the other night after that run," I tell him.

"I meant I'd actually stretch you out. I'll also give you a massage." Finn drops his hand to the base of my neck, and it's hard to hold back a groan when he adds a push of pressure with his thumb. "Doesn't that sound fun?"

It does sound fun.

Way better than spending the day alone and miserable, and I've *missed* him.

I've never missed anyone after a hookup before, but I can't get him out of my head.

When I laced up my shoes this morning, I thought about him.

When I wanted to give up at mile two, I thought about him.

He's in front of me, grinning like he doesn't have a care in the world, and I'm still thinking about him.

"Okay," I agree. "But this is the last time. There are rules about one-night stands turning into two-night stands. What happens when we accidentally get to a three-hundred-and-one night stand?"

"I guess we'll find out if that happens. Rules are meant to be broken, Margo, and I don't think three hundred and one nights with you would be the worst thing in the world." He winks, and we join his friends. "Is everyone in one piece?"

"Barely," Holden says. "I got a cramp at mile one and hobbled my way to the finish line."

"You still finished, and that should be celebrated. Rhett? How are you holding up?"

"Surviving," his other friend says. "I passed this ten-year-old when I was twenty yards from the finish, and it was satisfying to beat him."

"He's a child, Rhett." The woman next to him rolls her eyes then smiles at me. "Hi. I'm Jada, his wife."

"I'm Margo. Nice to meet you." I smile and shake her hand. "You didn't run?"

"God, no. I like being in the crowd. Preferably with wine."

"I think we're going to get along." I pull away from Finn so I can give Katarina a sweaty hug. "I cannot believe you won. That's incredible, Kitty Kat. You're amazing."

"Thank you." She grins and hugs me tight. "And I'm so proud of you. Sub-ten minute miles are damn fast."

"I learned from the best." I kiss her cheek and grimace. The ache in my legs is settling in, and I know I should stretch them out. "Ow."

"You okay?" Finn asks, and concern laces his tone. "What hurts?"

"Everything." I bend down and rub my calf. "I'm all right."

"I'm going to take Margo back to my place so I can make sure she's on the mend. Forgive me for bowing out of lunch," he says to his friends.

"You don't have to ditch lunch for me," I say, not wanting to create a rift in the group. "You should go with them. I'll survive. A hot shower will mend me right up."

"Nah. They'll be fine." He grins down at me, and I melt like a damn snowman in the summer. "They don't even like me that much."

"It's true," Holden agrees. "He's our least favorite one in the group."

"See?"

I glance at Kat, and she gives me an encouraging nod. I've never been in this position before, and I feel out of place. I've never seen someone a second time after agreeing it would only be the one time, and the nerves I didn't have the first night we were together start to show themselves.

For some strange reason, I care what this man thinks about me. I care that he wants to spend more time with me, and I care that he was there to hand me a medal at the finish line.

I've never been one to mix feelings with a quick bedroom rendezvous, but here I am, excited to have another chance to spend a couple hours with him.

"Okay," I say, wringing my hands together. I have to hold back a grin because I'm so damn excited for a few more hours with him. "Yeah. That sounds good to me."

After a round of goodbyes, Finn leads us to his car with an arm draped casually over my shoulder. I like how close he is and how warm his body is pressed against mine. He opens the passenger door and gives me a small bow.

"Seatbelt, please," he says when I get situated. I laugh when he jumps into the driver's seat and shivers. "I have seat heaters that should kick on in a second."

"Thank you for inviting me over. I'm sure I would've been fine on my own, but it's nice to have some company."

He reaches over and squeezes my knee. "I'm happy you're here."

Christmas music plays on the radio, and I find myself humming along. The drive to his house is short, and when we get there, it's my turn to shiver.

"I didn't realize how cold I was." I wrap my arms around my chest as he unlocks the front door. "I was sweating thirty minutes ago."

"The sweat dried, so it's cooling your body off." Finn points to my shoes. "Take off your clothes and leave them here. I'll toss them in the washer after I get you in the shower."

"You want to see me naked again, don't you?"

"Can you blame me?"

His grin is a lightning bolt to my chest, and I peel off

my running outfit until a pile of clothes forms at my feet. I roll my shoulders back and look at him. A flash of excitement zips up my spine when I catch his eyes raking across my chest and down my legs, and I stand a little taller.

I've never been shy about my body, but somehow, being here with him after pushing myself to limits I didn't know I could ever reach, I've never felt more beautiful. I've never felt so strong and powerful, and a surge of confidence thumps in my blood.

"Are you going to take off your clothes?" I ask. "Or are you going to gawk at me all afternoon?"

Finn hums and steps toward me, dipping his chin. He kisses my neck and my cheek and tucks a piece of hair behind my ear. "Would you think I'm a creep if I told you I dreamed about your body? If I got off to the thought of your curves and the little scar you have on your knee? You're the most beautiful woman I've ever seen, Margo, and I don't know what the hell I did to deserve you spending time with me."

His words strike a match inside me, and I'm not cold anymore.

I'm alive, awakened and invigorated.

I slip my palms up his shirt and roam my hands across his chest. "No," I whisper, standing on my toes so our mouths are close. "Because I dreamed about you too."

I dance my fingers to the waistband of his shorts and over his hard length. Taking a step back, I saunter down the hall to his bedroom. A glance over my shoulder shows me Finn is palming his erection and staring at my ass with a gleam in his eye.

His bathroom is warm, and I reach into the shower, turning on the hot water and waiting for it to heat up. Finn comes up behind me and bands his arms around my waist.

He pulls me flush against his naked body and nips at my ear with the sharp bite of his teeth.

"You're a tease," he whispers. I drop my head back in the crook of his neck and his hands move over my breasts. He plucks and pinches my nipples, and I groan. "I've wanted you since the minute you left my place the other day. Do I get to have you again?"

"Finn." I spread my feet apart and kiss his neck. "I'm rubbing against you."

"Doesn't mean I get to have you. Do I get to have you again, Margo?"

Taking the hand on my chest in mine, I guide him between my legs. He hisses when his knuckles drag across my entrance, and I groan when he teases me by pushing his pinky inside me.

"Yes," I manage to get out. "You can have me."

"Good." His hand drops away, leaving me frustrated and turned on, and I scowl. "I know, baby. I'm going to take care of you, don't worry. I want to make sure you're not sore first, okay?"

Damn him for being so nice.

Damn him for looking out for me.

Damn him for making me not want to stay away.

I spin in his hold and lift my chin so our gazes collide. "Fine. But you better fuck the life out of me after all that's said and done. I'm a needy girl, Finn. And right now, I need you."

SIXTEEN

FINN

KEEPING my hands to myself in the shower is a goddamn feat.

It's nearly impossible to concentrate on anything besides the water running down Margo's tits or the way her skin turns a pretty shade of pink from the steam surrounding us. I'm distracted by her long legs and the flex of her muscles when I drop to my knees and run the bar of soap up over her calves, but I survive.

Barely.

When she's clean and no longer shivering, I lead her to my room and help her onto the mattress.

"I forgot how soft your bed is." She sighs and gets comfortable on her stomach. Her wet hair sticks to her bare back, and I straddle her, dropping a kiss on her neck. "Are you sure you want to give me a massage when you could be fucking me? That sounds a lot more fun."

"If you can be patient, we'll get there. This isn't an either-or thing. I can take care of you *and* fuck you." I rub her shoulders, and she lets out a long groan. "Your muscles

111

are stiff, and the only way to recover and feel better is to get them loose and relaxed."

"It hurts, but it also feels so damn good."

"It's nice, isn't it?" My thumbs dig into the soft skin of her neck, and she turns quiet under me. "Some people think the most important part of exercise is the exercise, but they're wrong. It's the recovery. And you, my friend, are carrying too much tension to consider yourself recovered."

"That's the second time you've called me your friend." Margo groans again when I apply an extra push of pressure with my thumbs. "Are we BFFs now?"

"Isn't that the natural progression? We fuck first, then we're friends after?"

"Do you fuck a lot of your friends?"

I laugh. "Can't say I do."

"We can be friends," she mumbles. "Or fuck buddies. Whatever you want to call it, but only if you don't judge me for drooling. My god. That feels so good."

I like the idea of fuck buddies. That means I could have her again and again until I had my fill. The only problem is, I'm not sure I'll *ever* get my fill of her. She's too damn sexy. Too damn alluring, and every time I'm with her, I want to learn more about her. I want to find a way to keep her around a little while longer, which is crazy.

No one should feel this way after only hanging out two or three times, but here I am.

Fucking desperate for more of Margo Andrews and willing to do whatever I have to do to make that happen.

"It's a judgment-free zone. I promise," I assure her, moving my palms down and kneading her spine. It's easy to find the knots in her back, and there's a particularly nasty one on the left side of her body, below her shoulder blade. I press into it firmly, and it's embarrassing how hard

I get when she moans. "Exhale for me, Margo. There you go. How does that feel?"

"You have magic hands." Her words slur and her eyes flutter closed. She's limp and pliant beneath me, and I leave another kiss on her shoulder. "Can you keep going?"

"I could do this all day."

I take my time and do my best to work out all the kinks I find. When I reach her ass, I rub my thumb along the curve of her cheeks. Her legs part, spreading open on the sheets, and I graze my fingers over her pussy to find her wet.

"*Oh*," she breathes out. Her thighs shift wider and she lifts her hips off the bed. I take advantage of the new angle and part her with my thumbs, holding her open so I can see what I've missed out on the last few days. "I've never had a massage like this."

I wonder what she'd look like full of my cum. I wonder what it would look like dripping down her thigh. I'm always smart when I have sex with someone; protection is a necessity and nonnegotiable, but I'm close to throwing that rule out the window. I'm close to asking her if I could fuck her without a condom, just so I can watch my release leak out of her greedy cunt.

"Do you like it?" I rasp, moving over her entrance again and teasing her for a handful of seconds before I move lower to her hamstrings. She whimpers, and I'm not sure if it's from wanting me to slip my fingers inside her or from the pain. "Or should I stop?"

"More," she almost pants, and I increase the pressure. She buries her face in the pillows, a moan working its way up her throat. "God, that feels so good."

I glance down and stare at her with wonder as she lifts her hips then relaxes them against the comforter. She rubs against the navy-blue duvet before lifting again, and I realize she's getting herself off. Using the sheets as a toy, and that's the hottest thing I've ever seen.

"I really only wanted to take care of you," I say low in her ear. I reach for the bedside table and grab a condom from the box I put there in a fit of optimism thinking I might see her again one day down the road. "I promise I didn't have any ulterior motives."

"Somehow——" Margo's sigh turns into a soft laugh when she rolls her hips. I know she's going to leave a stain on the fabric, but I don't care. I'll be able to smell her cum after she's gone. Maybe I'll jerk off on the same spot so I can pretend like I'm fucking her without a condom between us. "I don't believe you."

"Look at the one who has ulterior motives. You're fucking yourself, aren't you? You don't need me." I open the condom and roll it down my length. I spit in my hand and rub my shaft to cover it with the moisture. "But I think you want me, Margo."

I drag the head of my cock through her pussy lips. I'm only teasing her, not fully sinking inside her tight cunt yet. I want her to work for it. I want to rile her up and hear her beg.

Margo gasps and lifts her hips, trying to sink back on my dick. I hold her waist and bring my hand down, smacking her ass and watching her skin turn a rosy red.

"*Fuck*," she draws out, and desperation clings to the word. "Finn. Can you—I've had—"

"Is this what you want?" I wrap my hand in her hair and give her neck a gentle tug. She arches off the bed and she gasps when I finally push inside her. She's tighter than she was the other day, not stretched out from my fingers or the Christmas tree ornament, and I almost blow my load right there. "It is, isn't it? God, Margo. You take my cock so well."

I pull out of her so we can adjust our positions. She pushes up on all fours and glances at me over her shoulder. Her eyes bounce to where we're joined, and she licks her lips. Slowly, in some magnificent form of nirvana that is her cunt, she rocks her hips back until I'm buried all the way to the hilt.

"Fill me up, Finn," she says, and my name is like a goddamn siren song. I'm useless when she reaches between her legs and starts to touch her clit. "Stuff me with your cock."

Fuck.

I've been with vocal women before, but never with someone like this.

She's so *sure* of herself, and the words flow seamlessly out of her like she's been waiting years to finally say them.

"Jesus Christ." I stare at the ceiling, needing to break eye contact out of fear I'll finish in five seconds. "You're doing so well, Margo. Taking all of me like the good girl you are."

That spurs her on, and she slams onto my cock. The bed shakes and I grab her hips, needing something to hold while she fucks me within an inch of my life. I swear the way my body reacts to her is like an acid trip; I can't remember anything. My tongue is heavy in my mouth and I can't speak. I need more and more and *more*, a goddamn addiction I don't want to stay away from.

"Are you going to come inside me?" she asks, and it's breathless. Like she's hanging on by a thread, just like I am. "I hope you are, because I really want to come on your cock."

I don't stand a chance when she grabs my hand and leads me to her chest so I can pinch her nipples. My orgasm rears into me and I grind my teeth. I fill the condom with my release and pulse inside her, her pussy walls fluttering around me as she comes, too.

"Holy hell," Margo sighs. She leans forward and collapses on the bed, causing me to slip out of her. "No one has made me orgasm like that before."

"Boys, remember?" I flop onto the mattress next to her. "I think you killed me. I got through the run just fine this morning, so it makes sense I'd meet my demise with your pussy."

She laughs and turns on her side to face me. "I wish I could've seen you finish."

"Did you miss it when I came inside you two minutes ago? We can record it the next go around if you want to watch it back."

"I'd be down, but I was talking about the race this morning. You've seen me finish twice, and I haven't gotten a chance to watch you."

I hum and rest my arm over her hips. "There will be more races. I'm sure you'll see me at another one."

Margo pauses, and I wonder what she's thinking. It looks like her mind is going a million miles per hour. "This was supposed to be a one-night thing, and it's turned into a two-night thing. Or, a night-and-a-half thing,"

"I guess fate had other ideas when it came to us."

"What—" She scoots closer, and I pull her against me so we're chest to chest. "It's just sex, right?"

I weigh her question.

It's insane to think because we barely know each other, but I could see myself spending more time with her. Going on a date or two or three. I could get to know her better, and from what I've seen so far, that could be a lot of fun.

"I think our first night together was just sex," I say carefully. "But I'm an open-minded guy. Are you interested in a relationship right now?"

Margo frowns, and I smooth over the line of wrinkles on her forehead with my thumb. "I'm not sure, to be honest. I like you. You're a good guy, but when you add in the age difference between us, it feels like sex is the only logical answer."

"It's not *that* big of an age difference."

"Sixteen years is a long time, buddy. You've done the parenting thing already, and I might want that one day. You own your home. I rent. You know exactly who you are as a person, and I'm still trying to figure that out. Why waste each other's time if we're not on the same page?"

"How about this? We spend the last week before Christmas hanging out and getting to know each other outside the bedroom. Then we can decide what we want to do going forward. If that's just sex, fine. If it's nothing at all, that's okay too. Let's not complicate anything before we figure out what this is."

My heart races in my chest, and I'm nervous to be saying this to her. It's like I'm clinging to any possibility of keeping her around, even if it means prolonging the inevitable moment we decide to go separate ways.

"One more week?" she asks, and I nod. "I'd like that."

I grin. "Yeah?"

"Yeah." Her smile is shy and reserved. I haven't seen this side of her before, and she blushes before burying her face in her hands. "Do we get to keep having sex?"

"Oh, yeah." I pull away from her and scoot down the mattress. I take off the used condom and tie it in a knot, settling between her legs. "I'm going to learn your middle name, but we're also definitely going to keep having sex. Get comfortable, Margo. I'm just getting started with you."

SEVENTEEN
FINN

ME

Are you busy tonight?

RELUCTANT RUNNER

I'm glad we upgraded to texting instead of randomly running into each other and falling into bed together.

Still not convinced you're not stalking me.

ME

For the record, you ran into me at the bar. So, technically, you were (are?) the stalker.

RELUCTANT RUNNER

Whatever you say.

What do you have planned tonight?

ME

Want to go to the Museum of Art and look at the decorated trees?

RELUCTANT RUNNER

That sounds like a date.

ME

It's not.

Trust me. You'll know if I'm taking you out on a date.

This is a friend enjoying the company of another friend in a holiday environment.

RELUCTANT RUNNER

I'm intrigued by the decorated trees. Are you going to wear a festive sweater?

ME

Of course I am.

RELUCTANT RUNNER

You have a drawer full of them, don't you?

ME

Two, actually. There are about 300 of them.

RELUCTANT RUNNER

I can't tell if you're joking or not.

Okay. Let's go see some trees!

Do you want to meet there?

ME

You still think I'm a serial killer, don't you?

RELUCTANT RUNNER

I'm putting a fork in my bag. Just in case.

ME

We can meet there. I'd never want you to feel uncomfortable.

Unless you were fucking yourself with an ornament.

RELUCTANT RUNNER

I can't wait to see your video next year where you discuss how only ceramic Christmas trees can be used for insertion, and only if they have flared bases.

IT'S SNOWING when I make it to the Museum of Art. I shove my hands in my pockets and spot Margo climbing the steps to the entrance. She looks damn good with her hair blowing in the wind and her pink cheeks, and I can't help but smile at the sight of her.

"Hi," she says breathlessly, and I bend down to give her a hug.

"Hey. How was your day?"

"Good. I went shopping with Kat—which was a disaster—then spent the rest of the afternoon on the couch watching trashy reality television." She laughs. "I'm normally more productive, but I'm taking advantage of being lazy these few weeks I'm off from school."

"As you should. I can't imagine how hard you must work during the school year."

"How was your day? Did you run fifty miles? Record any fun audiobooks?"

"I finished up the stalker one. It's a lot easier to get things done when you're not naked in a chair in front of me touching yourself, believe it or not."

Margo swats at my shoulder, and it's my turn to laugh. "What book do you have next on the list? A bodyguard romance? A basketball series? Maybe cowboys?"

"All appealing, but next is something totally different. It's a romance with rival meteorologists. They chase a category five hurricane together. And fall in love along the way, obviously."

"Whoa. That sounds fun."

"It does, doesn't it?" I lift my chin to the building. "Want to head in? Your hands are shaking, and I could use a hot chocolate."

"Let's do it." She loops her arm through mine, and I lead her to the entrance. "You're a hot chocolate guy?"

"I am, but it has to be made with milk, not water. And, speaking of milk, my favorite thing to drink after a run is chocolate milk."

"Wow. T.G. Lee should give you a sponsorship. Why chocolate milk?"

"It's good for recovery, and as someone who could run a hundred miles a week while training for a marathon, I need to recover the best I can."

"I still can't wrap my brain around how much you run and how *good* you are at it." She looks up at me as I scan our tickets into the museum. "Have you always liked the sport?"

"Yeah. I played soccer as a kid, and my coach constantly had to tell me to cool my jets when I was on the field. I took up track and cross country in high school, and I've stuck with distance running as an adult." I shrug and hold the door open for her. "It's therapeutic, to be honest. My life and my job force me to be mentally focused, and running is the only time I don't have to talk to anyone. I don't have to think. I'm not a person with responsibilities. No one is counting on me. I can lace up my shoes and just be."

It's so damn easy to talk to Margo.

I noticed that the first time we met; she's snarky and sassy with a bite behind her bark, but she's also kind and a good listener. Someone who leans into nonverbal communication with her nods and her smiles. Everything she's thinking is written on her face, and right now, her wide eyes and the soft and sweet curve of her lips tell me she likes what I'm talking about.

"You might be the most interesting man I've ever met," she says.

"Why? Because I put on sneakers and run?"

"That's one of the reasons." She rests her head on my shoulder and smiles. I like her there. I like how she fits perfectly in my hold and how my arm feels wrapped around her. For a split second, I wonder what it would be like to have her like this every night. To take her out on dates and show her off to the world. I like the thought more than I probably should. "You have so many cool things going on in your life. It's impressive."

"Don't be fooled. Until you came along, I was really just a boring guy who sat at home most nights." I point to a large tree in the corner of the main room. "My hospital decorated that one. I picked out the ornaments."

Margo untangles our arms and leans forward. "Artificial? That's a letdown."

"Tell me about it. I called a whole committee meeting about the reasoning behind needing a real one, but I was shot down. Artificial is the only way it'll last all season for the show." I tap the syringe and stethoscope ornaments. "We're going to put it in the hospital after New Year's to brighten the place up for the kids in the pediatric area."

"Wow. That's a great use for it, and now I'm totally onboard with the artificial decision. Was it your idea to bring it back for the kids?"

"Yeah." I rub the back of my neck and give her a sheepish smile. "It was."

"Such a nice guy. You sound like you really like your job. Especially if you help to bring holiday cheer year-round." She moves to the next tree and tilts her head to the side, assessing. "This one is fine, but your tree is much better."

"Did these people even put in any effort? And I do like my job. It's not always fun, but it's always worth it, you know?"

"That's how I feel about teaching. Some days, I'd rather do anything else because it's physically and mentally draining. But then my kids show improvements in their reading or make their first friend in the classroom, and all the negativity goes away."

"You get it." I drop my hand to the small of her back and lead her to the last tree on this side of the room. I'm finding any excuse I can to touch her, to be honest, and if I have to give a tour of every damn decorated Fraser fir in the building, I will. "Thoughts on this one?"

"Are you sourcing opinions for next year's entry?" Margo asks with a teasing smile, and the beam is a jolt to my heart.

It feels like I'm being shocked with an AED. Like I'm getting resuscitated after spending minutes flatlining. I've seen her done up in makeup and cute outfits. I've seen her stepping out of the shower with mascara under her eyes. I've seen her in the middle of the night, half asleep and smiling at me like she's far away in a nice dream, and one thing is true: she's so goddamn beautiful.

She's sexy and a goddamn tease, but there's something soft about her. Something loving, and it's making me feel like a teenage boy with my first crush all over again.

My palms get sweaty when she's nearby. I want to puff out my chest and do something stupid to keep her attention when she's looking at me. I crave her in a way I've never craved anyone else, which is exactly why I asked her to meet me in public instead of tumbling into my bed again—I want to get to know her, because I think there's something here. Something bigger and better than sex, and it has me really goddamn curious.

It's been a while since I've dated someone; two years, maybe?

I've had fun with other women. I've had the casual hookups and the quick encounters back at my place after a night at the bar, but none of them have ever held my attention this long.

Margo does, and she does it easily.

I like everything about her.

"Yeah." I clear my throat and tug on the collar of my snowman sweater. "We finished in third place this year, and anything less than first next Christmas is going to be a disappointment."

"Your tree was third? What the hell was first? Something sent from the North Pole?"

"Come here." I hold out my hand and she takes it, her slender fingers locking with mine. We wind our way through the rest of the entries from local businesses and big-name brands. I stop us in the last room toward the back of the museum, and point at the twelve-foot tree in the center of the space. "That one."

"Holy cow. They put a whole town on their tree?"

"Yup. Houses. Roads. A train that weaves through the branches. Check out the icicle lights. It makes it look like it's snowing."

"Okay, no offense to your *Grey's Anatomy* tree, but this is incredible." She walks around and stares at the masterpiece in awe. "It reminds me of this general store back home that decorates for the holidays. It's incredible."

"Where did you grow up?" I ask, watching her excitement as she touches one of the house figurines. "Is it a small town you'd find in a Hallmark movie?"

"Hardly." Margo laughs and moves back to my side. "I grew up in Michigan, and I moved to Chicago after college."

"Are your parents still residents of The Mitten?"

"They are. My dad is a pilot based in Detroit, and he snagged a five-day London trip over Christmas. My mom is joining him, so I'll see them after the holidays."

"No aspirations to be in aviation?"

"I thought about it. I like talking to people, but I prefer to be grounded."

"Any plans to leave Chicago in the near future?"

"Why?" She turns to face me with a sharp, sly grin. When she looks up at me, I have the urge to kiss her. To pull her into a hug so I can keep hearing about her hopes and dreams. "Would you be sad to see me go?"

"Yeah." I make a show out of looking her up and down. I'm committing parts of her to memory, like how her left hip pops out when she's trying to be sassy and how her hair has the slightest curl to it. "I would be."

"Well." She adjusts the hem of her skirt, and I want to run my hand up her thigh and along warm skin. I want to pull her into my arms and make her see there are good people in the world who can treat her better than my son. "I'd be sad to leave. Especially now. So I'm not planning to go anywhere."

I have no fucking clue what happens to us after next week.

Could we date and be serious about each other?

Would we do a friends with benefits thing until one of us decides to settle down with someone else?

That's a problem for down the road, because I tug her to me. I cup her cheek and rub my thumb down her jaw, grinning when she gives me a megawatt smile.

"Sounds like you enjoy spending time with me, Miss Andrews," I murmur.

"What can I say? Your sweaters have grown on me." She pauses and rests her hands on the center of my chest. "You've grown on me too, Mr. Mathieson."

I fight back a groan and drop my forehead against hers. "You can't call me that here. It makes me want to be young and stupid and yank you into a closet and go down on you."

Margo giggles, not sorry at all. "I'm going to grab us some hot chocolates." She stands on her toes and kisses my cheek. "If you decide you want to be young and stupid, you know where I'll be."

She pulls back and offers me a wink. I watch her saunter away, hips swaying from side to side, and I'm hit with the terrible fucking realization I'm going to miss her a hell of a lot after this is all said and done.

EIGHTEEN
MARGO

SWEATER GUY

Are you awake?

ME

Define awake.

I'm currently buried under a pile of blankets because my apartment is cold as shit, so yes, technically I'm awake, but I'm not happy about it.

SWEATER GUY

Not a morning person?

ME

I'm a mid-afternoon person. I really shine at two p.m.

Let me guess. You get up before the sun.

SWEATER GUY

Always. The world is a lot nicer before everyone wakes up.

> **ME**
>
> You're probably ready for lunch, aren't you?

SWEATER GUY

Not quite. I'm downstairs with coffee.
Figured I'd pump you with caffeine so we
could go for a run.

> **ME**
>
> How the hell do you have my address?
>
> And run? It's twenty-four degrees outside.

SWEATER GUY

Perfect weather for a jog.

> **ME**
>
> You might be certifiably insane.

SWEATER GUY

At least I have coffee.

> **ME**
>
> I'll take the caffeine, but the run is up for
> debate. I'm building four, apartment 623.
> Sixth floor.

SWEATER GUY

See you soon, late riser.

"I'M STILL TRYING to figure out how you know where I live. The thriller books and true crime podcasts would tell me I'm about to be a victim. Is this some method acting for another stalker romance you're recording?"

"I followed you on Strava. All your runs start and end here, so it was pretty easy to figure it out," Finn says.

"Wait." I frown. "You can see that on the app?"

"Mhm. I'm not one to tell you what to do, but you

should consider updating your privacy settings so it hides the first quarter mile of your workout. You don't want creeps following you places or learning your routines, and that information is readily accessible. I can help you do that, if you want."

Warmth blossoms in my chest. "You would do that?"

"I know how lucky I am to be a male runner. I've seen the shit women deal with: the catcalls. The harassment. The stalking. It makes me sick that you can't run with headphones because you have to be aware of your surroundings at all times. I don't have that kind of fear, and I recognize it's a privilege to run without having to be worried. I don't want anything to happen to you, Margo, and I want to make sure you're safe."

I lunge for him and wrap my arms around his middle. I bury my face in his shirt and inhale the scents I've come to associate with Finn: peppermint, the touch of cinnamon, and a hint of something spicy. I hold him, afraid if I let go, I'll wake up from the dream where this wonderfully considerate man is in my life.

"Thank you," I murmur into his chest. "And good morning."

"Good morning." He kisses the top of my head and I slowly pull away from him. "How'd you sleep last night?"

"Not bad." I yawn and gesture him farther into my apartment. I don't mention that I haven't slept nearly as well as the night we first hooked up. I usually like my space, a woman who craves her independence and the ability to do what she wants, when she wants, but I liked being in his bed with him by my side. It's been hard to get comfortable like that again, and I find myself missing him in the middle of the night. "Welcome to my crib, by the way."

"You're too young to know that show."

"I'm an old soul, Finn."

"I like your place." He smiles and looks around. His attention snags on the photos hanging on the wall, and he taps one of me and Katarina. "What the hell is happening here?"

"Oh god." I bury my face in my hands. "I was drunk in the back of a cab after an awful date with a guy, and Kat took that selfie of us when I was mid-rant about how I'm never dating again. I like how happy I look."

"Your smile is huge." Finn pries my hands away from my face and passes me my coffee with a grin. "Tell me why the date was so awful."

"He picked me up from my apartment."

"Wow. What an asshole. I hate him."

"With his *mom*."

"Fucking hell." He laughs and takes a sip of his drink. "Did she also chaperone you at the table?"

"No, but he wouldn't stop talking about how amazing she is. Don't get me wrong; I love my parents very much. I'll sing their praises to anyone who asks, but I started to think this dude was *in love* with his mom. His maternal fixation was *weird*. Oh. He also licked his fingers and dipped them in his water glass to clean them off... then drank out of it."

"On behalf of men everywhere, including my son, I apologize for the sins my gender has committed."

"Come on." I lean against the wall. "You've probably done something stupid on a date."

Finn wrinkles his eyebrows, deep in thought. "I'm not sure I have. I know that's subjective, but I haven't seen any of my dating stories on the AITA Reddit threads, so I think I've done a decent job. I can give you a couple of women's numbers if you want to ask for a breakdown on my behavior, though. They'll be honest with you."

The idea of him with another woman makes my skin prickle.

It's silly. He has a *son*—who I've slept with—with another woman. For all I know, he's fucking four other people right now because we haven't had a conversation about exclusivity or what the hell this situationship is.

But I don't like picturing him with his head between a blonde's legs. I don't like picturing him with his mouth on someone else's chest. I want him to do that with *me*, not them, and I fear I might have just climbed into a hole I'm not going to be able to get out of.

"That's okay." I sip my coffee so I can give myself a second to think. "Do you date a lot of people?"

"I haven't dated anyone in a minute, but I've had some physical relationships. I'm not an asshole, by the way. Everyone is aware of the parameters before we get started."

"You're not leaving a trail of broken hearts across Chicago?"

"I hope not. I'd never want to do that. What about you, Miss Andrews? I know my son was a prick, but what about before him?"

"I've dated some people. I've had a couple friends with benefits. I'm not sure where I land on the whole *settling down* thing, but I have time to figure it out."

"You have many years ahead of you."

"Did you tell Jeremy about us?"

Finn sets down his coffee and steps toward me. "Tell him what, Margo? That I've seen his ex-girlfriend naked? That I stripped her down in my hallway and fucked her on my kitchen table?" He runs his fingers down my thin sleep shirt and grazes over my hard nipples. "That I have her on audio saying *my* name, not his, when she came? No, baby. I haven't told him you're a slut for my cock and that's why one night turned into two times, then three, and after we finish our run, I'm going to make it four."

I almost drop my coffee when I moan at his words.

I love how vocal he is. How there's no doubt in my mind about what he's thinking or feeling.

I especially love how *filthy* he is.

At the museum two nights ago, he pulled me into a closet like he said he would and went down on me. He dropped to his knees, flipped up my skirt, and ate me out until he had to fold a large palm over my mouth to keep me quiet.

"Can't we have fun first, *then* run?" I dance my free hand over the front of his shorts, and his hard cock twitches against my palm. "You feel a little worked up."

"I'll make you a deal." He yanks on my hair and pulls my head back so he can kiss my neck. "For every mile we run, I'll give you an orgasm."

"What if we run ten miles?"

"Then it looks like we'll have a busy day."

"Wow. Who knew the promise of orgasms would be the reason I'd consider running a marathon? But you've read those romance books, Finn. Where the women come fifteen times like they're magical beings with unlimited orgasms. Pretty sure that doesn't happen in real life."

"Then we should test that theory to see if it's fiction or reality." Finn wraps his arm around me and squeezes my ass. "Go get dressed. And wear a tight sports bra. I want to watch your tits bounce."

"I THINK I'M DYING." I groan and shield my eyes from the glare of the sun. "How long have we been going?"

"Five miles." Finn hands me a bottle of water and I

gulp it down. "We're a mile and a half from your place. Want to keep going?"

The orgasm incentive is enticing, but my legs are heavy from the last few weeks of half marathon training, plus the two races. Finishing the morning with six miles is better than what I had planned, and I don't want to hurt myself.

I know Finn would never let that happen, but it's better to tap out while I'm ahead.

"Let's go home." I hand the water back over to him, and I haven't missed the way he's carried it this whole time in case I needed it. "You can go ahead of me if you want. I know I'm slowing you down."

"That's not true." We turn around and head down the riverfront pathway. "I'm enjoying this pace."

"I bet you are. It's practically walking."

"Hey." He pinches my side. "Enough of that negativity. Do you know what I tell Holden?"

"No." I settle into an easy jog and look over at him. "What?"

"Miles are miles, no matter how fast. All you need is a pair of shoes, and sometimes, you don't even need those."

"The sport is important to you, isn't it?"

"Every day I'm out here is a gift, and I want to have fun with it. Fast. Slow. Doesn't matter."

"That's a good perspective to have."

"That's what I'm here for: perspective and wisdom."

"Okay, all-knowing one." I laugh when he gently nudges my side with his elbow. "I don't hate running as much as I did four months ago. When I first started training, I'll admit it was out of spite and anger. But I've learned things about myself along the way, and that's pretty cool."

"It's really cool," Finn agrees. "Hey. I'm sorry for showing up at your place without asking. That was fucking weird. You didn't tell me I could be there, and I crossed a line."

Maybe I should've thought it was weird, but in the times we've spent together, I've never felt uncomfortable around him. I've never felt like I'm in danger or at risk of getting hurt. Everything has been so *good*, and for someone whose son was straight-up shitty to me, he's been nothing but incredible.

Finn was right about what he told me the time we were first together; he *is* a man. This isn't a game. There's no hidden agenda. We're two adults enjoying each other's company, and I'm not scared of him.

"It's okay," I say. "I had no idea Strava shared my location to the world, and it's not like you were some rando who followed me home one night. I'm not creeped out. I'm more impressed with your sleuthing skills. Katarina would be proud."

"Ah. So I'd have the best friend's approval? Sounds like a win in my book." He smiles and reaches over to touch my shoulder. "Really, Margo. I'm sorry. I won't show up unannounced again. I promise."

I kind of hate how much of a nice guy he is.

If he were an asshole, it would be easy to make an excuse not to see him anymore.

But now I'm looking for reasons to spend time with him. Doing anything I can to stretch out the minutes we have together, because I like being around him so dang much.

"I'll make sure to invite you next time. Or you could sleep over and be there in the morning. That wouldn't be unannounced." I stick out my tongue, and Finn laughs. The tension leaves his shoulders and he sighs in relief, like he was actually terrified I'd be mad at him. "What's our pace?"

"Cruising right around eleven thirty, Miss Andrews, with a mile to go. How're you feeling?"

"Tired but strong. It's a lot more fun to have someone to run with. Makes time go by way faster."

"If you ever want another running buddy, you know how to get a hold of me. We can even keep the orgasm incentive in place."

"Does this stretch into the new year?" I ask casually. "Or does it expire on Christmas?"

"No expiration date, but the orgasms can be off the table if you want. A run with a friend is always fun. It doesn't have to come with any benefits."

"Glad to know I have some options." We turn left, and the wind nearly knocks me over. "How do you decide to dress for these runs? I was freezing my ass off when we started, but now I'm sweating."

"I always underdress, but I keep my ears and hands covered. The more you run, the more you'll be able to figure out what kind of layers you want or need." Finn adjusts his beanie. "Should we grab some breakfast before we head back to your place? There's a diner six blocks up that does a mean stack of pancakes."

"I'm down. As long as it's not interfering with anything else you have going on today."

"I don't work until tonight. I'll take a nap before I head in, but I have a few hours. What do you say? Want to celebrate a good run with some delicious food?"

I glance over at him, and when I catch the way he's smiling at me with a lock of hair sneaking across his forehead and pink cheeks, I realize having breakfast with him sounds like the most fun thing in the world. It sounds like exactly the spot where I want to be.

I don't care that I'm sweaty. I don't care that my legs might cramp up when we're sitting in a booth. I don't care that my shirt is sticking to my body and my hair is out of control.

I'm so damn attracted to him, and I wonder if I'm crushing on this man, or if it's the endorphins talking.

"Let's do it," I say.

"Awesome." Finn tugs on my arm and pulls me to his chest. He looks down at me with a wide smile, and my heart skips a beat. "I was hoping you'd say that."

Crush, my brain screams.

Definitely a crush.

NINETEEN

FINN

RELUCTANT RUNNER

What are you doing tonight?

ME

For you? I'm free as a bird.

RELUCTANT RUNNER

You don't even know what I'm going to suggest!

ME

Doesn't matter.

RELUCTANT RUNNER

What if I'm going to ask you to go to a knitting class? Or to play bingo?

ME

All sounds fun to me. Is that what's on the agenda?

RELUCTANT RUNNER

No. I was thinking we could watch a Christmas movie. Or I could listen to you record another audiobook...

Do you have any other decorations I can ruin? Maybe a reindeer?

ME

I just laughed out loud. The guy behind me in line at the grocery store is looking at me like I'm an idiot.

I'll be home in 20. Come over whenever. And bring stuff to stay the night.

RELUCTANT RUNNER

A sleepover? Fun. Maybe I'll show up in a trench coat or something sexy like that.

ME

You could show up in a bag and be sexy.

RELUCTANT RUNNER

Be careful what you wish for...

I'VE SPENT every day since the 5k with Margo.

We're having a good time, and I like that she keeps wanting to see me. Some days we have sex. Some days we don't, and that's perfectly fine with me.

There might not be a plan for us after Christmas, but I'm enjoying seeing where this goes. We don't have any pressure on us, and I've fully accepted that no matter what happens between us, I'm going to be happy for the time we've shared together.

The knock on my front door comes after I've put away all my groceries, and when I open it and find Margo on the steps, a big red bow in her hair and wearing a literal pillowcase as a dress, I burst out laughing.

"What—" I wheeze and clutch my side. "The hell is that?"

"You said I'd still be sexy in a bag, so I decided to put that theory to the test." She rests her hands on her hips and does a twirl. "Well? What's the verdict?"

"You look like a Christmas present I want to unwrap." I tug her inside, out of the cold, and run my hands down the front of the pillowcase. "Aren't you freezing?"

"Pretty sure my nipples are going to fall off, but it's worth it." She bends down to unzip her boots and nudges them against the wall. "Hi."

"Hi." I pull her close and kiss her, smiling when she wraps her arms around my neck. "How was your day? Do you have a closet full of pillowcase dresses?"

"No, but a very informative YouTube video helped me craft this before I walked out the door. My day was good. Better now that I'm here with you."

"Ah. I like to hear that." I move my hands to her ass and cup her backside. "Have you eaten dinner?"

"Not yet. I thought we could order some pizza." Margo presses a kiss to my neck, and her tongue licks up my throat. "Later, though. There are some things I want to do first."

"Like?" I walk us backward to my office, wanting another show like I got the other day. "Is there something you need, Margo?"

"You," she says, and I kiss her again as we stumble into the room. "In a lot of different ways."

"You know where to sit," I murmur against her mouth. "And get comfortable, baby. We're going to have some fun."

"Oh, are we?" She pulls the pillowcase dress over her

head and drops it to the floor, leaving her in a lacy red number that has a dozen bows all over it. My mouth goes dry at the sight of her, and she smirks. "See something you like, Mr. Mathieson?"

"Fuck," I rasp. I'm instantly hard from seeing her, and it's never been like this with other women. One glance at her and I'm shoving my hand down my pants. Gripping my cock and stroking myself because she's so goddamn sexy. "You are exquisite."

Her face softens, and she sits in the chair across from my desk. She scoots back and lifts her legs, draping them over the arms of the chair. Her hand rests low on her stomach, and her eyes never leave mine as I nearly trip making my way to my chair.

"I like when you compliment me," she says softly. "I'm used to diving into the action, and I've never really felt seen before. You make me feel seen."

I'd throw the whole dictionary of compliments at her if I could. I'd call her every adjective under the sun if it made her smile like she's smiling right now.

"I'm never going to stop complimenting you." I reach for my desk drawer and open it, pulling out the order I had delivered earlier today. "Even when I'm on top of you. Even when you're on your knees in front of me. You are, without a doubt, the most spectacular woman I've ever been with in my life, Margo. And I don't want you to forget that."

Her breathing hitches, and she drags the strap of her outfit down her left arm. She stops just before she shows off her tit, and I almost whine at the tease.

"What's in that box?" she asks.

"I, shockingly, don't have any other vagina-approved Christmas ornaments in my house, so I got you a toy." I rip open the cardboard and hold up the plastic. "So you can fuck yourself while I watch."

"I don't think you're making the nice list this year." Her green eyes sparkle and she lifts her chin. "Will you open it for me?"

I have a disagreement with the scissors and curse until I finally get the plastic open. I toss the toy her way and she catches it, weighing it in her hands.

"I did some research. It, uh, has good reviews," I say, and I don't know why I'm suddenly nervous about all of this. "I can take it back if you don't like—"

Margo runs the toy across the front of her underwear. She drops her head back and groans when she circles her clit with the silicone head. "Will you read to me, Finn?"

"*Yes.* Yeah. Fuck yes." I grab the first script I can find on my desk and rip it open. "*Her eyes widen when she sees the mask I'm holding. A look of fear crosses her face, and I wait for her to tell me it's okay that we go down this path. She steps toward me and takes the knife from my hand. I suppress a groan when she touches the tip of the weapon against my throat, and the smile I give her is anything but nice.*"

"I don't want that done to me, but listening to it is really fucking hot." Margo pulls her underwear to the side and bares herself to me. She drags the toy across her entrance, coating the silicone in her arousal, and I'd give anything to taste her. Anything to get on my knees in front of her and worship her cunt the way she deserves. "Can you keep going?"

I sit back in my chair and unfasten the button of my jeans. I unzip the fly and put my hand down my pants so I can jerk off to her excitement. Her eyes track my movements. She grins and brings the toy to her mouth, wrapping her lips around the tip.

Fucking hell.

I'm starting to think this woman was made for me. The things she's interested in and the way she—

"Dad?" My front door slams shut and my blood runs cold. "You home?"

"Is that Jeremy?" Margo hisses.

"I don't know what the fuck he's doing here." I scan the room, panicked. I don't care that he knows Margo is here. I don't want him seeing her like *this*. He lost that privilege, and I'll be fucking damned if I'm giving him that opportunity today. "You need to hide. I'm sorry. I'm not embarrassed by you, but I—"

Margo stands, and I almost whine again. Her tits look fantastic, and I'm going to fucking *kill* my son for interrupting us. "Where should I go?"

There's no way in hell I'm making her climb out the window, and sneaking down the hall to my room is out of the question.

"Under my desk," I say. "He won't be able to see you from the other side."

"I've always wanted to be someone's dirty little secret." She rounds the corner of the furniture and gets on her knees. "Please be quick."

"If it were up to me, he'd already be on his way out the door. And I'm definitely taking his fucking key from him." I touch her jaw, and our eyes meet. "Hey. I'm not happy about—"

"I know." Margo kisses my knee and ducks her head so she's hidden. "Just so you know, I'm not a very patient girl, Finn."

"Christ," I grumble, shoving my dick back in my pants right as Jeremy makes his way to the threshold of my office. "Hey, Jer."

"You didn't hear me yelling for you?" He frowns and leans against the wall. "The fuck are you doing in here?"

"Work." I hold up the script and my eyes dart underneath my desk. "Are you good?"

"Yeah. Just haven't seen you in a minute and thought I'd stop by." Jeremy walks to the chair Margo was just sitting in and plops down. "Are you coming to Mom's for Christmas?"

"Yeah. Yup. I am indeed. What else did you need?"

"Wow. Every other time I see you, you're the one ragging on me for rushing off places. That's a little hypocritical of you, Pops."

I grind my teeth.

I usually love to hear what my kid is up to, but when I have the woman of my dreams inches away from me, the last thing I want to do is sit here and shoot the shit for an hour.

"Sorry. I have a lot on my mind and I'm behind on some reports I need to do for work."

"What's with all the microphones?" Jeremy looks around and frowns. "Looks like you're hosting a podcast in here."

"The hospital asked me to record some things for the website, so they sent equipment over." Out of the corner of my eye, I see Margo under the desk. She's staring at me, and her lips wrap around the toy again. My hand curls into a fist at my side, and I watch as she slowly works the silicone head into her pussy. "Jesus Christ."

"What?"

"Nothing. I—nothing." Margo grins. She drops her head back and starts to fuck herself, half the length of the toy disappearing inside her. "Just. Having a hard time remembering something."

"Are you having a stroke?" he asks. "You're freaking me out."

"I'm healthy as hell," I say, scooting my chair closer to

the desk so there's no chance he can see her. "What about you? Didn't see you at either of the races Run Chicago put on the last two weeks."

"Been busy." He grins and crosses his arms. "I've been seeing a couple of people, and time has slipped away from me."

"How's work? How's the dealership?"

I almost bite my tongue when soft hands work their way up my thighs. My fingers curl around the arms of my chair, and I don't know if I love Margo or hate her.

She traces the outline of my cock over my jeans, and it's damn near impossible to keep my mouth shut.

Love.

Definitely love.

There's no way she follows through with this, but another glance between my legs shows me her mischievous smile, and I know I'm well and truly fucked.

TWENTY
MARGO

I HAVE a feeling I'm going to be in big trouble when Jeremy leaves, but I'm having way too much fun to care.

Damn the consequences.

I hate having to hear my ex's grating voice. It takes me back to when I walked in on him and my co-worker and I had to listen to him try to explain himself.

For as much apologizing as he did in the moment, he never texted or called me after to try to get me back.

Funny how things work out.

With one hand on the toy, I run my other over Finn's hard length. I rub him through his jeans, and I can tell by the way his thighs flex and he scoots closer to the desk, caging me in, that he likes it.

"Work is good. It's always chaotic this time of year. Everyone wants to surprise their significant other with a new car, even though they're probably going to drive it back to the dealership the day after Christmas," Jeremy says.

I push onto my knees and let the toy fall out of my grasp. The rug muffles the sound of silicone hitting the hardwood floor. I turn my attention to Finn and use both hands to unzip his jeans all the way. I dance my fingers along his lower stomach and I'm delighted to learn he's not wearing any underwear.

I smirk and touch his cock, springing it free from his pants. Having been someone who sat in the chair Jeremy is in, I know there's no way he'll be able to see anything; the dual computer screens and microphones hide most of Finn's body from view, and the last bit he *could* see is hidden all the way under the desk.

It's safe to do whatever I want.

Feeling bold and reckless, I take Finn in my hands. I rub my thumb along the slit on the head of his cock, grinning when I find pre-cum there.

I like a lot of things about him, but one of my favorites is how easy it is to tell he's into me. He gets hard when I touch him. His eyes heat and he tracks my movements. He has to curl his hands into fists to actively stop himself from touching me sometimes, and for a girl who likes to know she's wanted, there hasn't been a second of doubt since I stumbled into bed with him.

Like right now. He reaches for me. His fingers dance down the line of my jaw and move to my hair, stroking the strands in the most reverent way. But then he *yanks*, his intentions clear, and I decide I'd like to play this game every day.

Finn and Jeremy are still talking. I hear something about horsepower and four-wheel drive, but I don't pay them any attention. My focus is on making the man in front of me feel as good as he's made me feel.

I stroke his cock up and down, wishing I could find an angle where I could take him in my mouth. Knocking my head against the desk and my ex finding out I'm jerking off his dad is *not* on my list of things I want to accomplish today, so I stick with my hands.

I'm slow and teasing, increasing the pressure and pace with every new question Finn answers. The vein on his forearm tucked under the desk is almost popping out of his skin, and I hold back a laugh when he folds his hand over mine, asking for more.

"I need to get back to work," Finn says, and it's strained. Like he's fighting an uphill battle he knows he's going to lose. "But I'll see you in a few days at Christmas, bud."

"Okay." There's a creak of a chair, and I wish I knew what was going on. Is Jeremy walking to this side of the desk to give him a hug? Is he already halfway out of the door? "Are you sure you're okay, Dad? Your face is flushed. Mom will kill you if you come over and get the twins sick."

"I—*shit*," he curses when I lean forward and lick up his length. I'm going to have a crick in my neck for days, but it's worth it for that reaction. "I just need some sleep. I'm fine. I promise."

"If you say so. Love you, Dad."

"Love you too, kid," Finn says, and footsteps retreat from the room. "Lock up when you leave, please."

"No problem," Jeremy calls out.

Not more than two seconds after the front door closes, I'm being pulled to my feet and put on the cool wood of the desk. My underwear is being ripped and my bra is unhooked. A microphone crashes to the floor, and Finn's mouth is on mine. Warm, bruising, he kisses me like he's claiming me, and in a way, I wonder if he is.

"You fucking tease." He bites my neck and pinches my nipples, the dual sensations causing heat to race through my body. "I almost came in my pants in front of my *son*."

"It's a shame you didn't." I tug the belt loops of his

jeans and shove the denim halfway down his thighs. I wrap my legs around his waist and lean back on my elbows. "How would you have explained that to him? 'Sorry about that. Your ex-girlfriend has her hand on my cock.'"

Finn bends down and takes my breast in his mouth. He sucks on my nipple and moves his hand between my legs. He pushes two fingers inside my pussy without warning, and I cry out. "Look how fucking wet you are. Fucking yourself with a toy. Trying to suck me off. All while he could've seen. You're a slut, Margo."

I whimper when he pulls out of me and pushes his thumb against my clit before giving it a light slap. This is rougher than he's been with me, a trust established and a safety net laid out after a few times together.

It's mind-blowing. Exquisitely sensual and so damn *hot*. I never want it to end.

"Do you know what would make me more of a slut?" I pant. I reach for his cock and drag the head of it across my entrance, just like I did with the toy. "Is if you fucked me without a condom. If you filled me with your cum and made me walk home with it running down my leg."

Finn freezes, and I panic.

I've overstepped.

I've said the wrong thing.

I've never had sex without protection before, but the idea of *him* being the one to break my streak seems fitting. Some cosmic plan from the universe that's been in place all along.

"I'm sorry," I whisper. I try to scoot away, but his other hand touches my neck. Gently wraps around my throat and tips my head back so I have to look at him. "That was completely out of line and—"

"Are you on birth control?" he asks, and it's the deepest his voice has ever been. It's like gravel, some rough and desperate sound I've never heard escape from him before. "Margo. Are you on—"

"Yes. *Yes*. I am. I—" I swallow and lick my lips. "This would be my first time without—"

"My first since I was a teenager."

There's a moment of silence until Finn kisses me again. Until he eases me back onto my elbows and puts his hands on my knees.

"Hold your legs wide open for me, Margo," he says, and I race to loop my arms under my thighs. "Thatta girl. You're so good for me, aren't you?"

I've fucked myself with a Christmas tree in front of him, for fuck's sake, but this… this is different.

Dirtier, almost, because he looks me up and down, and a coy smirk settles on his mouth.

"Need to get you a little wetter." Finn drops to his knees and presses his thumb against my clit again. I jerk forward, electrified by his touch. "Hold still."

I do my best to not squirm. To stay in place and enjoy what's happening. But then he brings his mouth close. With his eyes on me, he spits, and the saliva lands on my pussy.

Finn takes off his jeans and kicks them away. He peels off his shirt and I'm left studying his beautiful naked body as he lines himself up with my entrance.

"Fuck me," I whisper.

"This is going to be rough." The crown of his cock works inside me, and I gasp. Stars take over my vision and I drop my head back, ecstasy already building in my blood. "I'm not going to be nice." A rock of his hips buries the first fourth of his length in me, and I moan. "But I want you to remember I'm going to take care of you after, okay?"

I nod. It's a pathetic acknowledgment, and when he pulls out of me entirely, I'm afraid I haven't said enough.

"W-what? Finn, I—"

"Hush, Margo." He bends down and picks up the toy I was using. "Open up."

My lips part, and he puts the silicone head in my mouth. I sigh and suck on it like I would if it were his, like I would if it were real, and he lets out a shaky breath.

"Fuck. It's different when I get to watch you like this." Finn turns the toy to get it deeper in my mouth, and tears prick my eyes. "That's enough. You're going to make me come and you're not even touching me."

I pop the toy out of my mouth, proud. He lowers the fake cock to my pussy and grips my thigh as he works the first half of it in me. I moan and open my legs wider, excitement coloring my skin with Finn's sharp laugh.

"I'm going to take care of you. Don't worry." He pushes the whole toy inside me, and I gasp. It's not as big as his cock, but it's big enough. "Work for it, Margo. Let me watch your tits bounce. *That's it*. Look at how bad you want it."

I've never been so intimate, so *personal* with someone before, and where I might feel shame, I don't. I feel nothing but pleasure working its way up my spine. The sensation is heightened when he touches my neck. When he adds pressure to my windpipe and I grin, on top of the world.

My hands drop from my legs to the edge of the desk, holding on so I can find momentum and do what he asks.

The room goes blurry as I settle into a rhythm that brings me overwhelming bliss. As his hold on my throat turns a touch tighter. As an orgasm starts to show itself, the white-hot nirvana comes closer and closer with every rock of my hips. With every one of his whispered, *that's it. Look at you. The next time we're together, I'm using this in your ass while I fuck you.*

It's too much. It's not enough. It's everything I've ever wanted behind closed doors, the marks on my body an indication of getting exactly what I've so desperately craved.

"Finn." His name tastes like heaven and my movements turn frantic. I'm close—*so close*—and I've never been so needy for release before. "I'm going to—"

"I know you are. It's going to feel so good, isn't it? I can't wait to watch."

I squeeze my eyes closed and the orgasm barrels through me like a tornado. "*Fuck.*"

I'm gasping for breath. Convulsing on the desk and sobbing as Finn doesn't let up. He doesn't relent, keeping me full and stuffed while he touches my clit. While he rubs a circle over me and makes me come again, his laugh a wicked sin in the crook of my neck.

"Dirty girl. Making a mess in my office. That will be our secret too," he says, and I whimper when he pulls the toy out of me. "Open your eyes, Margo, and look at me."

My eyelashes flutter open, and I see that the toy is drenched. I expect him to tell me to lick it off, but when his own tongue runs up the length of the silicone from base to tip, I almost come a third time.

"Holy shit," I whisper. "You—that—" I swallow, and a million new fantasies race through my head. "Is that—"

"Something I like?" He turns the toy and licks the other side, keeping his eyes on me. "Usually? No. With you? I'd be up for negotiations."

"*Fuck,*" I say again, but I don't have any time to process how *indecent* it is to watch him because now it's the real thing. Now he's sinking into me without any barriers between us, and I lose my mind.

It's even better than it was before. I can feel every vein, every ridge of his cock as he drives into me, again and again, until there's not an inch of space left.

"You are——" Finn rests his forehead against mine and I can feel the sweat on his skin. "So fucking tight. So fucking perfect. Holy shit. I'm never fucking you with a condom again."

"I thought you said you weren't going to be nice?" I tease, but it's like the words are my last breath. Like I'm never going to be able to say anything ever again, because he stands on his toes and jerks his hips, getting deeper than he's ever been. "*There. That* is what I want."

The intensity he puts into the snap of his thrusts is unimaginable. The way he moves his hand back to my throat is dizzying. It's rough. It's messy. It's loud.

I knock over a jar of pens when he takes my nipple in his mouth. I almost scream when he yanks me to the end of the desk and finds a new angle. I chant his name when he pulls all the way out of me before slamming back in, his sharp nails leaving pink welts on my legs.

The last of my coherent thoughts drift above the room and float out the window, but one remains: I could do this every day and be happy. This could be my life, and I'd be so damn satisfied.

It's the sex talking, yeah, but it's the way he soothes the sting after. It's the way Finn goes from biting my nipple to lapping at it gently. It's the way he holds me with all his strength so I don't fall, so I don't get hurt, and how he looks at me like I'm the most precious thing in the world.

"Margo," he slurs, sounding exactly how I feel: utterly exhausted. He's using me, a vessel for his pleasure, and I can't be bothered to care because it's all so magnificent. "I'm going to—do you want me to pull out? Where do you want me to finish?"

"I told you I'm a slut," I whisper, running my fingers through his hair. I drop my hand to his ass and stroke over his cheeks, increasing the force of his thrusts when I urge him forward. "Fill my pussy with your cum, Finn. I want the world to know whose whore I am."

"*Fucking hell*," he groans, and it's the only warning I get before he cants forward. Before his movements slow and his warm release coats me, an intimacy I've never experienced cloaking me in a swarm of emotion.

I glance down. My mouth parts in awe when he slowly pulls out of me and a trail of cum lands on my thigh. My nipples harden when he swipes through the remnants that escaped and shoves his fingers inside me, curling them in the cruelest way.

"Oh my god." I squirm, overstimulated. Worked up but too tired to chase another orgasm. "Finn, I can't—"

"Not wasting a fucking drop," he mumbles. He covers my pussy when he pulls out his fingers, then taps it twice. "There we go. Perfectly stuffed and perfectly full."

Perfectly yours, I want to say, but I keep that to myself.

I don't know if I should be mortified or turned on by what just happened, but I'm leaning toward the latter.

"That…" I groan when I try to stretch out my legs. Everything is sore. Everything hurts. I need a hot shower and to stretch out in bed. "I liked that very much."

"Yeah?" Finn looks at me. His cheeks are red and his eyes are wide. "I wasn't too—"

"No. It was perfect."

"Good. That's good." He licks his lips. His eyes rake over my body again, and he touches his cock. "How is it that I'm ready to go again? What are you doing to me, Margo Andrews?"

"The same thing you're doing to me. I'm not usually this easy to work with, but you make it work just fine."

Finn looks like he wants to say something else, but he doesn't. He lifts me in his arms and kisses me softly, gently, as he walks us to his bedroom.

After he washes my hair and cleans me up, he sets me in his bed. He curls up next to me and whispers how wonderful I am. How beautiful I am, and I drift off to sleep, thinking this might be the best Christmas I've ever had.

TWENTY-ONE

MARGO

"WHAT ARE YOU DOING TONIGHT?" Katarina asks me over the phone. "Something fun, I hope. Christmas is like, two days away, and you shouldn't be home alone during the holidays."

"I'm hanging out with Finn. We're making cookies at my place," I tell her. "And I think he's making me dinner? Maybe he's bringing me dinner. He wasn't totally clear."

"You're spending a lot of time with him. How is it going?"

"Good. We're having fun."

"Mhm. And by having fun you mean hanging out every night and smiling ear to ear?"

"That's exactly what I mean." My phone buzzes and I pull it away to see a message from Finn. "I have to run, Kat. I think he's here."

"Text me if things get too awkward and you need me to bail you out. I might be eight states away and in my childhood bedroom, but I'll break all the driving laws to kick his ass."

"I appreciate your dedication to my safety, as always." I

laugh and wipe my hands on a dish towel. "I'll keep you posted. Tell your mom I say hi and Merry Christmas."

"Will do. Love you, Margo."

"Love you, too, Kat."

I toss my phone on the counter and hustle to the door. When I open it, I burst out laughing at Finn's outfit.

He's wearing a Santa sweater that has a fuzzy beard and a hat with a bell. His pants are covered in reindeer and he's holding a plastic bag and a small box.

"Hey," he says with a grin. "Sorry I'm a few minutes late. The Thai restaurant was busy tonight, and I had to wait a little longer than usual."

"Wow." I lean against the doorframe and grin. "I have you saved in my phone as Sweater Guy, and you're really proving that name to be right."

"You're in mine as Reluctant Runner."

"Ah. A match made in heaven." I take the bag from him and stand on my toes. Before I can kiss his cheek, he's turning his head and kissing my lips, ferocity behind the press of his mouth as if he didn't see me yesterday. "Come on in."

"Thanks." He shrugs out of his coat and kicks off his boots. "It's fucking freezing outside."

"You ran in shorts and a t-shirt the other day. I thought you liked the cold."

"I was moving my body, Margo. Waiting for takeaway to be ready while being stationary is basically hell."

"Your huge-ass sweater didn't keep you warm?" I tease, and he gives my ass a light smack. "Careful! I'm sore from the thorough fucking we did yesterday."

"I'm sorry. Do you forgive me?"

"Only because you brought food. What did you order for dinner?"

"A little of everything," he says, and we walk down the

hall to the kitchen. "I can't believe you've never tried this place before. Their red curry is to die for."

"I don't want to die." I unload the bag of food on the table in the corner and point at the plates I set out. "Could you bring those over? And speaking of dying, how was work?"

"That was a morbid transition." Finn scoops up the plates and puts them next to the cartons of food. "It was fine. Busy, but fine. Sorry I answered your text so late. We had a couple of emergencies we had to work through and—"

"Hey." I lace my fingers through his and squeeze his hand. "You don't have to apologize for being busy. You were at work. Not purposely avoiding me."

"I'd never purposely avoid you." With a tap on my hip, he sits down and rests the box he's been carrying in his lap. "Did you have a good day?"

"I did. I worked on some lesson plans for next semester and looked at the curriculum for the biology class at the local high school." I shrug and open a carton of white rice. "I think I might apply to a few positions over the summer. Why not?"

"Holy shit. That's amazing, Margo." He beams at me. "I'm so proud of you."

His words light me up, and I can't help but smile back. Those feelings I've been having for Finn seem to manifest and hit me square in the chest when he holds my gaze, and I know I'm attracted to him.

I know I have a crush on him, and I want to find a way to keep him around after the holidays.

I want to see him in the spring when the weather turns nice and the snow melts, and that is a terrifying thought I'm not sure how to voice.

"Thank you," I say, embarrassed but grateful for his admiration. "I figured, why not?"

"Why not is right." He adds some spring rolls to his plate and takes a bite of his food. "You know we're watching a Christmas movie tonight after we make cookies, right?"

"I figured we would after we didn't get to it the other night. Which one did you pick?"

"*Die Hard.*"

"You're joking. That's not a Christmas movie."

"Debatable, but I am joking. *National Lampoon's Christmas Vacation* is the obvious choice because it's a goddamn classic."

"That's the one where the kid licks the lamp post, right?" I ask, and he looks at me, horrified. "I'm kidding."

"You almost gave me a damn heart attack."

"We wouldn't want that." I lift my chin to the box on his lap. "What's that?"

He sets the package on the table and nudges it my way. "I got you a present."

"What? I didn't get you anything."

"I don't need anything. It's nothing special, and it required some assistance from Katarina."

"You recruited her?" I wipe my hands and pick up the box. I give it a small shake and frown at the rattling noise inside. "There's nothing alive in here, is there?"

"Nope. But it is fairly fragile, so be careful."

Intrigued, I peel back the tape and slowly unwrap the gift. When I get all the paper off, I crumple it into a ball and chuck it at his head. "You would be an expert gift wrapper."

"Blame my mother. She used to teach a class around the holidays, and I was always her assistant."

"She sounds lovely."

Finn smiles. "She is. Go on and open it."

I pop open the top of the box and stare at the gift inside. "What—is this—"

"Your medal and bib from the half marathon? Yeah. It is. I wanted to frame them for you so you could remember your first race. Even if you never run another one, you have *that*, and it's something you should be very proud of. The back of the medal is engraved with your time on it. I almost included the form you signed in the medical tent, but I decided to leave that out. Good memories only."

How do I tell him the medical tent is one of my favorite memories? How do I tell him that meeting him that day was the best thing that's happened to me all year?

My nose stings. I brush my thumb under my eye and sniff. "Finn. This is…" I shake my head, unable to voice how meaningful this gift is to me. "I'm sorry. I don't know why I'm crying. A guy has never gotten me a gift before, and this is incredibly thoughtful."

"Hey." He sets down his fork and stands. Lifting me in his arms, he switches our positions so he's sitting in my chair and I'm in his lap. "I should be the one apologizing. I can't believe no one's gotten you a gift, and I'm honored to be the first."

"When did you even take this? You've been here one time, and the pockets in your running shorts are way too small to shove this inside."

"Katarina stole it for me when she was hanging out with you a few days ago. I got it engraved yesterday and wrapped it up before I headed over."

"Wow." I run my fingers down the edges of the glass frame. "I never thought I'd have a medal like this, and now I can show it off. Where should I put it?"

"Up to you." Finn smiles. "It's your accomplishment, Margo. Celebrate it however you see fit."

"In the living room." I jump out of his lap and hurry around the corner. I set the frame on top of the electric fireplace and admire the shrine. "That's perfect."

"I like it," he says from behind me, and I'm not surprised he followed me. "It looks great."

"Seriously." I turn to face him and tug on his sweater. "Thank you. This might be the best thing I've ever gotten."

"My pleasure." He cups my cheeks and cradles my face in his palms. "You have been the most unexpected surprise, Margo Andrews."

When Finn kisses me, I feel it everywhere.

It takes up residence in every part of my body, and it's a joy, a warmth I want to feel again and again.

It's soft and sweet. Like we're two lovers who have spent a lifetime together, and I put my whole soul into the press of my mouth.

I wrap my arms around his neck and run my fingers through his hair, close to him but still feeling like we're too far away. My toes curl and my heart hammers in my chest.

I know I need to talk to him about what I'm thinking and feeling. It's only fair, and I don't want to get too caught up in a thing that has an ending or results in us walking away down different paths, because I know I would regret letting him go.

His hand roams down my body and slips under my shirt. His fingers fan out across my stomach and his thumb strokes my skin. I want him so badly.

Tonight.

Tomorrow.

The day after that.

"This might be my favorite Christmas ever," I say against his mouth.

"Touching me in my office while I talked to my son,

who had no idea you were on your knees under the desk, really amped up the holiday cheer, didn't it?" He bites my bottom lip and dips his hand under the waistband of my sweatpants. I like that I don't have to dress up for him. "I knew you enjoyed that."

"I did enjoy it." I gasp when his touch teases across the front of my underwear. "But I meant meeting you. Then meeting you again. All of it. This has been a whirlwind, and I wouldn't have it any other way."

"Me neither." Finn drops his hands and sighs. "We're putting a pause on this until we finish dinner. You've been doing a lot of running and need your calories. Especially if you're going to burn more when I fuck you later."

"Oh, is that what's going to happen?" I ask.

"There has to be a joke in there about being a ho-ho-hoe."

"Wow." I grin and take his hand in mine. "That was the stupidest thing I've ever heard."

"Maybe." He kisses my forehead and I sigh. "But you like it."

"Yeah," I whisper, clutching his shirt like my life depends on it. "I do."

TWENTY-TWO
FINN

I'M in a shit ton of trouble.

I like this girl.

I like this girl a lot.

I like her when she's sitting across from me and asking for more food. I like her when she's laughing at my sweater or a stupid joke I tell.

I really like her when she has flour on her face and dough on her fingers from the cookies we're making. When she smiles at me, it's a punch to my gut. It's a reminder of how beautiful she is, how fucking *fun* she is, and I want to bottle it up so I can see it whenever I'm feeling sad or lonely.

"Hey!" Margo exclaims when I wrap my fingers around her wrist and lift her hand in the air. "What are you doing?"

"Making sure everything tastes okay." I bring her pointer finger to my mouth and wrap my lips around it. I suck the dough off her nail and lick down her finger. "Wouldn't want you to end up poisoned."

"What if I wanted that bite?" She tugs her finger free

and puts her own mouth around it. "It's rude not to share."

"Sorry. That was selfish of me." I grin and use my thumb to wipe away the flour from her cheek. There's even some in her hair, and I can't wait to get her into the shower after we eat the dessert we've made. "Your kitchen is a mess. You're a mess. Did any of the dough actually end up in the oven?"

"After you finished eating it all, I think we managed a dozen cookies. Maybe one or two less."

"And we're going to eat them all when they come out."

"Can your rocking six-pack sustain that much sugar?"

"What are you talking about? It's the perfect way to carb load." I grab the mixing bowl and drop it in the sink. "I'll clean this up."

"No way. I'm guilty of contributing to this disaster, and you're my guest. I'm not going to make you do all the work."

"Tag team it?" I ask, and Margo grins.

We work in tandem cleaning up and make small talk between wiping down the counters and rinsing out the measuring cups. Margo talks to me about the places she used to travel with her dad when she was a kid, the layovers she got to experience and the stamps she has in her passport. I mention the volunteer work I do at the animal shelter on the rare weekends I have off and how I've been thinking about adopting a dog to help fill the void of living alone and not having anyone to come home to.

Half the flour on the counter lands on my sweater when I try to wipe it up. I drop my head back and laugh when Margo draws a snowman right next to the bell of Santa's hat on my chest. I put my palms on the back of her sweatpants, leaving handprints on her ass she doesn't bother to clean off.

The oven beeps when I put the tablespoon and teaspoons back in the drawer next to her dishwasher. I grab the oven mitts, taking out the cookies and setting them on the stove.

"They look delicious." I turn off the oven and pull her to me. "Nice job, chef."

"Pretty sure this is all because of you. I would've burnt them all and had nothing to eat." She grabs a cookie off the sheet pan and blows on it. "Want to take the first bite?"

"Gladly." I sink my teeth into warm chocolate chips and sigh. "God damn. That's delicious."

Margo pops the other half in her mouth and hums in agreement. "So freaking good. It's not your first time making Christmas cookies, is it? You were way too quick to whip out that tree cookie cutter."

"I'm a damn expert at this point. Last year, there was a gingerbread house competition at work, and I took first place. You should've seen the decorations I piped."

"Sounds like you missed your calling to be on *Great British Bake Off*. You're too busy saving lives to be a pastry chef."

"One of your comfort shows?" I grab another cookie off the tray and hand it to her. I smile when she bites down on a reindeer's head. "What else do you like to watch?"

"Anything that makes me laugh. Romcoms. *Ted Lasso*."

"God. *Ted Lasso* is fucking brilliant. When Jeremy was a kid, he played soccer with a bunch of five-year-olds. I got tapped in to be the head coach, but I was let go after a month for being too competitive." I lick the pad of my thumb and brush a piece of cookie away from the corner of her mouth. "Sorry. Is it weird to talk about him?"

"No." She shakes her head and shrugs. "He's part of

your life. He was, unfortunately, part of mine too, but that doesn't mean you can't mention your son. The only time I've seen you be a parent is when my hand was on your dick, but you're a nice guy, Finn. And I bet you're an incredible dad."

I don't know why that makes my chest hurt, but it does. Maybe because, in less than two weeks, I've come to value Margo's opinion of me more than I value other people's. Maybe because I want her to keep thinking I'm a nice guy. Maybe because I want to give her the whole fucking world and ask for nothing in return.

I knew I was physically attracted to her when I saw her from a distance, back when she was dating Jeremy. But now that I've gotten to know her, I've learned she's this incredible force of a woman I'm emotionally attracted to too.

And fuck if there aren't differences between us: an age gap. Life experiences. Hell. We might even have different goals and where we see ourselves in ten years, but I cannot deny the pull between us. The electric chemistry we have, and even if it's for another month or another year, I don't want to give that up without giving this a try.

"Thanks," I rasp, and I rest my hands on her hips. "Do you have any plans for Christmas Eve tomorrow?"

"Nope. Katarina is out of town, and with my parents across the Atlantic Ocean, it'll be me and a movie marathon on the couch."

"Come to my place. I have the tree and the decorations. It's supposed to snow. It'll be nice."

"Are you sure?" Her eyebrows wrinkle and she touches my jaw. "Don't you want to spend some time alone after work?"

"No. I want to spend it with you."

Her gaze collides with mine. She chews on her bottom

lip, and I'd give my entire life savings to know what she's thinking.

"Okay," Margo says slowly after a beat. "I'd like that."

"Yeah?"

"Yeah. Your sweaters are a lot more fun than sitting by myself."

"I knew that's what sold it. I'll cook dinner and—"

My phone buzzes on the counter, and I glance at it. Layla is FaceTiming me, and I look back at Margo.

"It's my ex. Jeremy's mom. Mind if I take this?"

"No." She smiles and pats my chest. "I'll get the TV ready so you can have some privacy."

"You can stay here." I draw her closer to me and rest my chin on her head. "You don't have to run away. Besides, she'll probably call me a dimwit or something, and you might want to hear that."

Margo laughs. "Fine. But keep me out of the frame."

"Got it." I position the screen my way and answer. "Hey, Lay."

"Finny. I'm going through the list for Christmas and —" Her eyes bounce from whatever she's holding in her hand up to me. "Is that flour in your hair?"

"What? Oh. Yeah." I touch the lock across my fore- head and laugh. "I'm making cookies."

"Cookies, huh?" Layla grins. "With who?"

"A friend."

"A friend," she repeats. "And is this friend pretty?"

"Yeah." I turn my attention to Margo, who sticks out her tongue. "Prettiest woman I've ever seen in my life."

"Wow. You haven't smiled like that in ages. I'm clearly interrupting something, so I'm going to make this quick. I have you down to bring mashed potatoes and the turkey for dinner. Is that still the plan?"

"You know it, Laylacakes. If you think of anything else

you need, shoot me a text tomorrow and I'll swing by the store when I'm out. Oh. I got the twins a gift, by the way."

"You didn't have to do that."

"Course I didn't. I wanted to."

"You're too nice for your own good. Thank you, Finny. They can't hold themselves up, eat or think, but they're going to love it. You're the best."

"I try." I flash her a smile and play with the ends of Margo's hair off camera. "Rhett, Jada and Holden are coming too, by the way. I figured that was okay, since we're going to have enough food for a small army."

"The more the merrier."

"I have to run, Lay. I'll see you at two on Thursday?"

"Sounds good. See you then! Say hi to your pretty friend!" Layla blows me a kiss and hangs up.

"You two get along," Margo says, and I silence my phone. "And it's nice you spend Christmas with her family."

"At first, it was for Jer. We wanted him to have that cohesive family unit, you know? When Jeremy went to college, we kind of just kept spending the holidays together. I've brought people. She's brought people, but we've learned co-parenting is a hell of a lot easier when you like the person you're working with."

"That sounds nice. She sounds nice."

"She's great." I pop another bite of cookie into my mouth. "Ready for a movie?"

"Yeah, *friend*. I am," Margo teases, and I narrow my eyes.

"I think you might get in trouble for that one, Miss Andrews."

"Well." She dusts off her hands and slinks away from me. "If you can catch me, Mr. Mathieson, I'll let you punish me."

I blow out a breath and grip the counter. "I'll give you a five second head start, baby, but I won't be nice if I win."

"The naughty list is way more fun." Margo pulls off her shirt and drops it on the floor. With no bra, her tits spill free, and I groan. "Ready?"

"I may not make it to Christmas Day if you keep walking around like that."

With a wink and a devilish grin, she says, "Then we better have all the fun we can tonight."

TWENTY-THREE

MARGO

OF ALL THE places I could be on Christmas Eve, curled up with Finn on his couch is exactly where I belong. The wood on the fire crackles. The glow from the Christmas tree lights bathe the room in swatches of color. Outside, it's been snowing for the last two hours, and a winter wonderland covers the streets of Chicago.

It's perfect.

"What's the best Christmas gift you've ever received?" He lifts my hand in the air and locks our fingers together. "Besides mine."

"Someone thinks highly of himself."

"I'm not the one who cried."

"Wow. Low blow there, Sweater Guy."

"I'm kidding. I like that you're comfortable enough around me to show emotion. It's cute."

"You just earned some points back." I rest my leg over his and look up at him. "I think the pink and sparkly bike my parents surprised me with when I was seven is the best gift I've received. I rode that thing around our neighborhood until the wheels fell off. What about you?"

"When Jeremy was six, he painted this family portrait in art class. He spent so much time on it, and even though I had eight fingers and he had three legs, it was really special."

"You strike me as a sentimental guy who keeps all the cards he's been sent for the holidays. Do you still have the portrait?"

"It's in a box in my closet. Doubt I'll ever get rid of it."

"You shouldn't. It's special."

"It is." Finn wraps his arms around my middle and kisses my forehead. "Are you hungry? I bought stuff for burgers."

"Maybe we can eat later." I pull away from him and throw a leg on either side of his hips, straddling his lap. He rests his hands on my waist and drags his thumb across my skin, under the flimsy cotton of my tank top. "I'm not hungry yet."

"And if I am?" He sits up so he can brush his mouth against mine. He tastes like the bourbon he poured us an hour ago. "I'm fucking *starving*, Margo."

We both know he's not talking about the food. He lifts his hips, and his hard cock presses against my ass. I smile and rest my hands on his chest, rolling my hips until his grip on my sides turns rough.

I scoot down his thighs and take off my shirt. Finn blows out a breath and holds my breasts in his hands, a look of wonder stuck on his face. "Then you should eat."

"You really are the most beautiful person in the world." He rolls my nipples between his thumb and forefinger before giving them a pinch. It's my turn to exhale, a shaky puff of air that turns strangled when he gently flips our positions so I'm on my back. "I could stare at you all night."

"You can do that. If you want."

Finn holds himself above me and kisses me. It's passionate and slow. His tongue grazes against mine and his teeth sink into my bottom lip, an assault on my senses when he puts his hand on my stomach and traces the outline of my ribs.

"I want to do so many things with you," he says softly, and there's a world of possibilities behind it. "If you'd let me."

"Like what?"

He doesn't answer, telling me with his mouth and his hands instead of his words. He tugs on my lounge pants and pulls them down my legs until I'm naked on the couch. He kisses my neck, my chest, the spot under my left breast that's secretly sensitive.

I sigh and relax into the cushions, a hand in his hair and the other on my stomach as he takes his time with me.

Everything we've done up to this point has been fast and heavy. A burning flame that turns into a wildfire. This is gentler. A spark, not a blaze, and I savor the way he pays attention to every inch of my body. I revel in the way he puts a pillow under my ass and adjusts his position so he's between my legs.

"Margo," he croaks. My name cracks on the second syllable, and he stares at me. "Can I have you?"

"You can always have me," I answer, and Finn shakes his head. Moves his hands to my ass and brushes his fingers along the valley between my cheeks, and my skin prickles with excitement. "*Oh*. Yes. Yeah. That's… I'd like that."

"You said you've done it before?"

"Yes." I lick my lips and squirm. Anticipation builds low in my stomach, and I shift on the pillow. "A while ago. You won't be able to fuck me tonight, but you could—"

"That's plenty. I just want all of you."

He kisses me again and touches all over my body. The methodical way he moves is torturous, and he never lingers in one place for too long. I'm panting by the time he reaches between my legs and slowly rubs my clit.

The slick sounds of my arousal fill the quiet room when he pushes inside me and fucks me with two of his fingers, but I'm not embarrassed. I'm ecstatic. Craving more of him and already teetering on the verge of euphoria.

"You've done it before?" I ask, and a wave of nerves hit me as he slips another pillow under my backside.

"It's my favorite thing."

"Why haven't we done it yet?"

Finn pauses. He shifts on the couch so he's lying between my thighs, and he looks up at me. "Because I like you, and I never wanted this to be a quick fuck."

My heart races when he wraps his free fingers around my right ankle and rests my foot on his shoulder. He does the same with my left, bending my knees, and I think I might be burning alive.

"Want to watch you while I do it," he mumbles, and I nod, wanting to watch him too.

He sucks on his finger and dips his head. That alone is indecent enough, but then he ghosts over my back entrance and I drop my hands to the couch, holding on wherever I can grasp.

The fingers in my pussy curl, and a burst of adrenaline pounds in my blood. I groan and sink into the sensation, relaxing with every flick of his wrist.

"Ready?" he asks, and I nod.

I'm not prepared for the stretch his first knuckle brings me, and I hiss. I throw my head back and squeeze my eyes shut, doing my best to adapt to the new feeling.

"Give me a second," I say, and he kisses the inside of my thigh. He rubs his cheek against my knee and rocks his hips into the couch.

"Baby," he breathes out, and it's full of lust. "I wish you could see how good we look together. I wish you could feel how tight your ass is. *God*. You're going to make me come."

"A little more. Can you give me a little more?"

"Whatever you want. You're doing so well, Margo. Going to go to my second knuckle, okay?"

"Yes." My throat is full of dust and my entire body tingles. When he reaches the end of his finger, the pain settles to pleasure. The uncomfortableness is natural, *welcomed*. "*Move*, Finn."

He pulls the finger in my ass all the way out before pushing back in at the same time he adds a third one to my pussy. I groan, impossibly wet and deliriously full.

I know it's not going to take long for me to come. Not when he's figuring out a rhythm, alternating between in and out and knocking my world off its axis. His breath is hot on my skin. His words are muffled against my leg, but I catch a few of them: *beautiful. Perfect. I don't deserve you*.

It's a new level of intimacy for me, and when he licks my clit, his tongue doing that circle I love, my world explodes into a million pieces.

"Shit." A tear runs down my cheek and I gasp, trying to get my bearings but feeling like I'm on the verge of passing out. "Your fingers—"

"Imagine what it's going to be like when it's my cock." Finn keeps his finger in my ass, and I'm close to begging him to start again. To do *something*, because he's *everywhere*, and I'm not sure I can take anymore. "Gonna fuck your cunt with that toy while cum drips out of your ass."

Christ on a fucking cracker.

How can this be the same man who compliments me?

Who looks at me with a dopey smile like I hung the moon? The juxtaposition between his bedroom side and his real-world side is making my head spin, and I don't know which one I like best.

"Are you going to fuck me tonight?" I challenge, and he withdraws his finger, much to my dismay. He sits up and yanks off his shirt, his pants following shortly after. "That's more like it, Mr. Mathieson."

"You drive me out of my mind." Finn pulls the pillow out from under me and throws it at the wall. He crawls over my body until he's above me, and he wraps my hair around his wrist. "Suck, Margo. Get me nice and wet."

I open my mouth, and he puts the tip of his cock on my tongue. I smile around the head and take him to the back of my throat as another tear escapes from the corner of my eye. I keep my attention on him and lick his shaft. A smile forms when he drops his head back and groans.

I put the energy from my orgasm into bringing him close to the edge. I fondle his balls, cupping them in my hand, and I'm delighted when he tugs on my hair and pulls me off of him.

"Enough." His voice is hoarse, and he bends down to kiss me. "Keep doing that and I'll finish in ten seconds."

"Wouldn't be the worst thing. We have all night," I murmur, and his laugh is a sweet sound.

"Next round." Finn moves back down the couch until he's between my legs. He taps my knee, and I spread my thighs, giving him space. "Jesus, Margo. You're my favorite person in the entire world."

Two weeks with him, and he's my favorite person too. I start to tell him, but the words fall apart on my tongue when he sinks into me. When his hips snap and he buries his cock inside me, a slower pace than he normally settles into.

I think he's trying to draw it out. Trying to make it last as long as he can, because he's gentle and sweet. Making love, not fucking, and I like this side of him. I like the considerate way he touches my cheek. How he breathes out an exhale before driving into me again. His whispered praise and the way I can see him fall apart bit by bit until he's hanging on by a thread.

"Inside me," I tell him in a hurried tone. "It's the only place I ever want you to finish."

"Don't have to tell me twice." He touches my throat and his fingers drum against my windpipe. "I can't hold on much longer, baby. Your cunt is too—"

"So don't." I scratch my nails down his chest, and he moans. "I want to see it, Finn. I want to feel it."

That's all it takes.

With a final look at me, he slams home. The couch shakes and I gasp as his release spills inside me. I run my hands up his back as he calms down, and when he stills, I touch his jaw.

"*Fuck*," he whispers. "Am I in heaven?"

"No. Still here with me." I smile. "You okay?"

"Every time with you is the best fuck of my life."

"I agree with that." I push up on my elbows and tilt my head toward him. He pulls out of me with a wince, then kisses me. "You're so damn good at this."

"What? Sex?" He laughs and climbs off of me, collapsing on the other end of the couch and touching my calf. "I'm serious. It's never been this good before. We work well together."

"I guess we do. You know how you asked me about the best Christmas gift I've ever received?" I reach for him, and he takes my hand in his. "I think I'd like to change my answer to you. You are the best gift, Finn."

"Come here, sweetheart," he says, and I move to him

like the tide going out to the ocean. "You are, without a doubt, the best gift I've ever received."

I rest my head on his chest. His heart is racing, and the beat matches mine. I could stay like this forever. In his arms, content and happy. And when he kisses my forehead, I think he could too.

TWENTY-FOUR

FINN

I WAKE up on Christmas morning with Margo wrapped around me. I look down and smile at her messy hair and the marks I left on her neck last night.

I don't need any presents under the tree.

She's the best thing I could've asked for.

I run my hand down her arm and lean forward to drop a kiss to her forehead. She stirs and her eyes flutter open, looking up at me with a sleepy grin.

"Hey. What time is it?"

"Eight. Merry Christmas, Margo."

"Merry Christmas," she says around a yawn, stretching her arms above her head. "Why are you up so early? Please don't tell me you're coming back from a run."

"No running today. I just woke up. Sleeping in is nice." I play with the ends of her hair and tug on the sheet so I can see her tits. "So are those."

"This is sleeping in for you? You are such a weirdo." Margo buries her face in my bare chest, and I grin. "You're heading to your ex's house later, right? Probably with another sweater, I'm guessing."

"Yup. Dinner over there. I'm going to get the oven going for the turkey, but you should stay in bed."

"That's okay. I'll get out of your hair so you can get going with your day." She yawns again and throws the covers back. "I'll take an Uber home."

"Stay," I tell her before I can think twice. "You should come to dinner."

Margo blinks at me. "You're kidding, right? You want me to go to dinner at your ex's house where *my* ex, who is your child, will *also* be? That sounds like a fucked up soap opera."

"We don't have to tell anyone we're sleeping together."

"Pretty sure that's going to be the automatic assumption, Finn, given I'm a decade and a half younger than you." She stands and grabs one of my T-shirts to throw on. "I don't think it's a good idea."

I scrub a hand over my face. This conversation isn't going how I'd hoped, and the last thing I want to do is push her away or make her feel weird. "Can you come sit with me for a second?"

She eyes me warily and sits on the edge of the mattress. Her knee presses into mine, and I rest a hand on her thigh. "What's going on?"

"Look, Margo. I've had a lot of fun with you the last... however many days it's been."

I can't tell if time is flying by or inching forward. Every night with her passes in a second. Every hour I'm away from her drags like a month. I've never felt this way before, and I've never wanted to own a time machine more so I can keep going back and redoing all the minutes I get to spend with her.

"The sex is incredible, isn't it?" she asks.

"It is, but I meant I've had fun doing everything else with you. The museum. Meeting Katarina. Making cook-

178

ies. I know it's only been two weeks, tops, but I like you. I think you're funny and kind and hot as hell, and I don't..." I drum my fingers on her leg. "I don't want to stop seeing you. I want to keep spending time with you."

Margo sucks in a sharp breath. "You do?"

"I do. And I know it might be complicated because of my son, and I want to respect your boundaries, but I also don't want him to be the reason I don't get to see you anymore."

"What..." She swallows, and I track the bob of her throat. "Are you talking about dating? Exclusive fuck buddies?"

"I don't know what label it should be, just that I want to be with you and only you. I want—" I laugh and shake my head. "This is so stupid. I want to kiss you on New Year's Eve and I want to wake up with you on New Year's Day. I want to celebrate your birthday and Valentine's Day. Arbor Day, too."

"You don't even know when my birthday is," Margo whispers.

"No. But I want to learn it. I want to learn everything about you."

"That might be the most romantic thing anyone's ever said to me." She touches my jaw and drags her nails over the stubble I'm growing out. "Can I tell you a secret?"

"You can tell me anything."

"I'm scared by how much I like hanging out with you," she whispers. "I've been afraid to admit it to myself, but the more time we spend together, the more I think this could be... *something*. And I'm not just saying that because you're the first person to give me attention since my breakup. I'm just fine being independent and on my own."

"That doesn't surprise me at all."

"I'm saying it because you're nice and thoughtful and

probably the best man I've ever met." Her laugh is shaky, and I want to pull her close. I want to give her the fucking sun and every star in the sky. "I'm just... I'm worried we're at different points in our lives. We can't deny the age difference between us. What if in two or three years you want to settle down with someone more mature? Someone who has more life experience and knows the difference between a Roth and a Traditional IRA."

"I'm not sure even I know the difference."

"You know what I mean," she says.

"Who's to say you won't want to settle down with someone younger who isn't going gray?" I challenge. "Hell. We might get in a car accident tomorrow and not have two or three years together."

"Nothing says Happy Holidays like another morbid discussion of death."

"I'm serious." I pinch her thigh, and she grabs my hand. I link our fingers together and sigh. "I like you, Margo. I think about you when you're not with me. I miss you when you're gone. I want to keep getting to know you."

"This is the most mature conversation I've ever had with a man, and I want to make sure I answer appropriately," Margo says, and I grin.

"Sorry. Should I have sent a 'u up?' text instead?" I ask, and she tackles me onto the mattress.

"You make me laugh. You make me happy. I want those things with you too, Finn, but I need you to go slow with me. I want to do this right. You have far more relationship experience than I do, but I want to learn. I want to learn with *you*."

"We can go as slow as you need. Label. No label. I don't care. Which means you should not feel any pressure to come to dinner this afternoon. We don't need any sort of trial by fire."

"No." She shakes her head. "I want to go. Let's do it."

"Are you sure?"

"Yeah. I mean, who knows what's going to happen down the road, but for right now, I want to be a part of your life, Finn. And your life includes Jeremy. I told you I wasn't in love with the guy, and that's the truth. I can get through a holiday dinner with him." Margo pins me with a look, and her grin is mischievous. "But you have to be the one to tell him about us."

"Even if I don't tell him, he could probably figure it out. The hickey I gave you last night leaves very little to the imagination."

"My whole body is covered in marks from you. And my ass is sore as hell."

"Is it?" I reach to her back and rub her ass cheek. "Shit. I'm sorry."

"Don't apologize. It's a good kind of sore. As in, we should do that again. Immediately. Very soon."

I laugh and give her a light smack. "Let's get through Christmas with my family first. I don't want you walking funny because you're wearing a butt plug around my best friends." I hum, and my grin matches hers. "On second thought, that might be fun."

"Feels like we need to graduate to two fingers before a butt plug, Finn. Seems like the logical progression of anal play." She pats my chest and rolls off of me. I turn my head to look at her, and I'm struck with how fucking gorgeous she is.

Even with her messy hair. Even with sleep in her eyes. Even with chapped lips and my shirt on inside out, the wind gets knocked out of me at the sight of her.

"What's wrong?" Margo asks. She touches her face and

frowns. "I have makeup under my eyes, don't I? I bet I look like a sleep deprived raccoon who keeps getting railed by the hot older guy so she can't catch up on not being exhausted."

"Railing a raccoon isn't on my holiday to-do list, but you don't look like that at all. You look stunning."

"Stop it."

"I'm serious." I grab her wrist and stop her from covering her face. "Best way to wake up on Christmas morning."

She rests her forehead against mine and kisses me. "Are you going to keep talking to me like that a month from now?"

"Yup. Six months from now, too."

"Well. I guess I should get up and get ready so I can help with the turkey. I can't show up to our first event together empty-handed."

"First event together, huh?" I grin. "I like the sound of that, Miss Andrews."

"Go put on your Christmas sweater. And let me borrow one so I don't look like a total Grinch."

"Don't worry. I'll give you the merriest one in my drawer."

TWENTY-FIVE

MARGO

I'M A NERVOUS WRECK.

I'm trying to project confidence, but when we pull up to his ex's house, I panic.

"Hey." Finn shifts the car into park and taps my knee. "You okay?"

"I'm good. I had a lot more confidence when we were at your house, but I'm okay."

"We don't have to go in."

I appreciate his ability to stay calm under pressure, and I appreciate that he's not forcing me to do anything. It's one of the reasons why I like him so much: I feel safe when I'm with him.

I take a deep breath and look over at him. Finn is watching me, and his concern makes me smile. "I want to go in. It'll be good to close this part of my life and move on. With you."

"Look at you being all cute. Miss Independent knows all the right things to say."

I laugh and lean over so I can kiss his cheek. "Maybe

Miss Independent was just waiting for the right guy to come along."

"I see my cheesiness has rubbed off on you. If Jeremy gives you a hard time, I'll kick his ass."

"You'd do that for me?"

"I'd do a lot of things for you, Margo, and putting my son in his fucking place is one of them."

"Whoa." I smile and climb out of the car. I scoop up the big bowl of mashed potatoes we made together and hold it close to my chest. "That's hot."

"What is? Defending your honor?"

"Yeah. Maybe we should do some role-playing where you go into protector mode."

Finn's eyes flash with heat. He walks around the car and wraps his arm around my waist, careful to not disrupt the covered turkey he's holding. "That can be arranged. How about as a reward for getting through dinner?"

"Now you're talking." We walk to the house decorated with icicle lights and reindeer in the lawn. "Remind me your ex's name?"

"Layla. You'll like her. And you've met Holden, Rhett, and Jada. The allies are all on your side."

It reassures me, and when we head into the house without knocking, my nerves abate.

"Should we take our shoes off?" I ask in the foyer, and he nods.

"Yeah. We don't want the crawling babies to slip on a wet spot and hurt themselves. That's something you have in common."

"Wow." I kick off my boots and use my free hand to flip him off. "Look who has jokes. Does that sweater make you think you're funny?"

"I am funny, and I can see you trying not to smile." He

presses his lips to my forehead and starts down the hall. "Merry Christmas!"

I follow him into the kitchen. A beautiful blonde with long hair hugs him and laughs.

"There he is. Merry Christmas Finny," she says, but her attention moves to me. She lights up and grins. "And who is this?"

"I'm the pretty friend. Margo," I say, and Layla grins. "It's so nice to meet you. Thank you for letting me spend Christmas in your home."

"Oh, of course. Welcome." She hugs me next, then hurries back to the stove. "I figured there was more to that friend story than Finn let on."

"A lot more." Finn sets the turkey on the counter and I put the mashed potatoes next to it. "Might as well get this out now so dinner doesn't turn into a screaming match. Margo dated Jeremy for a few months. They broke up after he was a dick."

"Not surprising. That kid thinks he's god's gift to the world sometimes." Layla huffs and shakes her head. "Our son's infidelity aside, how did you two meet?"

"It involved me collapsing at the finish line of a half marathon. Not my finest moment," I admit. Finn pulls me close to his side and rests his chin on top of my head. The gesture feels so normal and natural, like we've acted this way in front of people a hundred times. "Then there was another random run-in at a bar, and now here we are."

"This just made my entire day. If Jer tries to act like an asshole, let me know. I have a toilet that needs to be cleaned in the guest bathroom, and I have no problem grounding him like I did when he was a teenager," Layla tells me, and I laugh.

"I appreciate it. I'm hoping we can all move on and enjoy the holiday. It's no big deal. No one's done anything wrong—well, I mean, *he* did, but Finn and I didn't." I shrug and relax into Finn's arms. "I don't care what Jeremy thinks."

"I like you a lot." Layla smiles and lifts her glass of wine my way. "Keep her around, Finny."

Finn curls his fingers around my chin and tips my head back. His eyes meet mine and he smiles. "That's the plan."

The front door slams shut, and I jump. Footsteps echo down the hall, and Jeremy walks into the kitchen. "Mom. Where is—" He spots me standing next to Finn. His eyes widen, and he freezes. "*Margo?*"

"Hey, Jeremy." I offer him a tentative smile. I'm waving the white flag, and the sooner we get past this, the better. "Merry Christmas."

"What the hell are you doing here? You're not here to… *fuck*. Please don't tell me you're trying to get back together with me."

I lift an eyebrow. "After you cheated on me? I'm all set."

"She's here with me," Finn says, interrupting us. His voice is sharp, some authoritative tone I haven't heard him use before. I love the deep growl that comes from the back of his throat. I love how his hand tightens on my waist. I love how he doesn't stop showing me affection just because his son is here.

"What do you mean *here with you?* Wait." Jeremy's eyes bounce between us. He bursts out laughing. "You two are fucking? Are you serious? She's *my* age, Dad."

"Fucking. Among other things. Is that a problem?" Finn asks.

"A problem? It's weird as fuck. And Margo never struck me as a wh—"

"Watch your fucking mouth when you're talking to her," Finn snaps, and I shiver. "We're not playing that game. It's not weird. It's not creepy. We met. She didn't know who I was. We spent time together, and we like each other. We're adults. It's consensual. Keep your comments to yourself, or say them to me. Not her."

Holy angel on top of the Christmas tree.

Forget role-playing.

That was the hottest thing a man has ever done on my behalf.

Nothing will ever top it, and if we weren't surrounded by his family, I'd be pulling Finn into the pantry to show him how much I appreciate him standing up for me.

"Jesus, Dad. Is this why you were acting so weird when I was over the other day? Because you've been messing around behind my back?"

"Behind your back?" Finn laughs, and it's anything but humorless. "You cheated on her, so you lost your opportunity to have an opinion on this. End of discussion."

"Who wants an appetizer?" Layla asks as she holds up a charcuterie board. "Or a drink?"

"I'll take a drink," I blurt, hurrying over to help her on the other side of the kitchen. "I'm so sorry for causing any issues."

"Please. The only issue is my egotistical son who thinks the world revolves around him." Layla pours me a big glass of wine and smiles. "I'm sorry he did that to you. I have no idea where he learned that kind of shitty behavior. Finn has never and would never—"

"I know." I smile and sip the Chardonnay, grateful for a distraction. "I didn't get that impression from him. It's only been two weeks, but he's so attentive and thoughtful."

"That's how he's always been: a nice guy who will go out of his way to make you smile. But he's smiling too, and I'm so glad to see him so happy. He's never brought a woman over for the holidays, and that tells me he must be serious about you."

"Yeah." I hide my smile with another sip of my drink. "I'm serious about him too."

Finn and Jeremy exchange a couple more words with each other that I can't hear. With a pointed look from Finn, Jeremy rolls his eyes and glances my way.

"Sorry, Margo," my ex says. "I didn't mean what I said."

"That was the most half-assed apology I've ever heard, but you can try again later." Finn clasps his son on the shoulder and grins at me. "Who's hungry?"

TWO HOURS LATER, full from a delicious meal and fun conversation, I pick up my empty plate and take it to the kitchen. I set it in the sink with the rest of the dishes, but before I can turn on the water to start cleaning up, Jeremy slides up next to me.

"Hey," he says.

"Hello."

"I'm sorry for cheating on you. I got caught up and enjoyed the thrill of doing something I shouldn't be doing. It wasn't personal."

While I appreciate his apology, it's not the part of our relationship that hurt the most. Being told I couldn't do something—like run a half marathon—stung, and I don't want him spreading that kind of negativity to other women.

I doubt I'll get through to him, but I want to say my piece and move on from all of this.

"You said I'd never be able to run a half marathon," I tell him, and he frowns. "Do you remember that?"

"Vaguely."

"You said someone like me would *never* be able to finish a run that long. Guess what? I did, and I kicked its ass. It's where I met your dad, so I guess I should be thanking you for your lack of faith in me. Because of your doubt, I'm happier than you could've ever made me. I found a man who believes in me. Who makes me want to keep running because he's so supportive, no matter how much slower I am than him. Words hurt, Jeremy, and if you tell people what they can't do, you're never going to keep anyone around."

"Wow. You actually ran a half marathon?"

"Yup." I cross my arms over my chest. "In two hours and twenty-two minutes."

"That's impressive." He sheepishly runs his hand through his hair. "I'm sorry for doubting you. That was shitty of me."

"It was shitty of you, but I'm glad you did. I like your dad, and I'd like to keep seeing him."

"Is there a problem in here?" Finn asks from the door-way, and I look his way.

His Christmas sweater has a stain on the front from where he dropped mashed sweet potatoes while helping to feed Layla's twins. His eyes twinkle, and he's smiling at me like he hasn't seen me in years.

"We're good," I tell him, and his beam stretches wider. "Just catching up."

"Catching up? If you want to strangle him for a second, I'll look the other way."

"No." I laugh and look back at Jeremy. "That won't be necessary. Thanks for the apology. I appreciate it."

"No problem." Jeremy sets down his plate and slips out of the kitchen, careful to avoid the glare his dad is tossing his way.

"Hey." Finn walks to me and hugs me tight. "Was he an ass to you?"

"He apologized, and I think all is well."

"Good. If I had to pick sides, I'd pick you. Obviously."

"Isn't there a saying about blood being thicker than water?"

"Not when your blood is a dumbass mid-twenty-year-old who can't keep his dick in his pants."

I laugh and rest my cheek on Finn's chest. I'm warm from our meal and two glasses of wine. I'm happy and relaxed in his hold. "Everything is okay. I'm glad I got to be here, and I'm glad we got that confrontation out of the way. I'm glad I get to be by your side."

"Think you'll come back to another gathering with the gang?" he asks.

I hear the hopefulness in his voice. The hint of excitement and the shadow of anticipation about what my answer is going to be.

"Yeah," I whisper. I play with the lights sewn into his sweater and smile. "I'll be back. For the food. For the company. For your eight hundred Christmas sweaters I haven't seen yet. For finding out what clothes you like to wear when it's warm out." I pause and look up at him. "For you."

His face softens. He brings his mouth to mine, and I hold his collar. "Want to know a secret, Miss Andrews?"

"More than I want anything else in this world, Mr. Mathieson."

"This is the best Christmas I've ever had."

I stand on my toes and grin. "Best Christmas ever."

EPILOGUE

Margo
Eleven months later

"THIS IS MORE overwhelming than spectating Chicago." I elbow my way through the crowd near the New York City Marathon finish line to get in front of the metal barricade blocking the course from non-runners. "How are you not freaking out right now?"

Holden laughs and steps to the side so I have space. "You'll get used to it after you go to your third or fourth World Major. This is your life now. The only thing better than New York is Boston. I can't believe Finn didn't run this year because you two were on a Mediterranean cruise. Where are his priorities?"

I know he's only teasing me; almost a year of dating Finn, and his friends have become my friends. His family is my family, and we all hang out, alternating between apartments for game nights and movie nights. Last week we were at Katarina's place, and I swear Holden pretended to forget his keys upstairs so he could spend more time with her.

It's cute he thinks we didn't notice.

"Weird. It's like Finn loves me or something," I say.

Holden drapes an arm around my shoulder. "He definitely loves you."

Gosh, does he.

He whispers those three words to me every day—in the middle of a speed workout when I'm regretting lacing up my sneakers and trying to chase him down.

At night when he comes home from the hospital and kisses me like the world is ending tomorrow.

This morning in our hotel room before he headed out for his race, curling up and wrapping his arms around me for an extra two minutes because he said he was going to miss me too much when he left.

Finn has encouraged me and motivated me in so many ways over the last eleven months. He's helped me be a better runner. A better teacher and a better person. Everything with him by my side is so damn *fun*, and I never thought ending up in a medical tent would change the trajectory of my life.

Jeremy took a few days to come around to the idea that Finn and I are together, and he honestly doesn't care. I don't hang out with Finn when he's around, but we're cordial enough to attempt Christmas together this year without any insults.

It's a start.

Everything has been so *good* lately, and watching him pass by at mile twenty-six of the marathon he's spent months training for is the perfect way to head into the holiday season.

"How's he looking?" I ask, and Rhett taps on the tracking app he's using.

"He's still with the leaders. There's a pack of seven of them that came through twenty-three together. Finn said if he was with the front group at 5k to go, he'd have a shot at being the first American to cross the line."

"I bet he does it." Holden jumps up and down, and I'm not sure if he's cold from the November New York air or excited. "He's in better shape than ever."

"I'm going to pretend like I helped with that," Katarina jokes. "Our early morning speed workouts are what made him even faster this year."

"It's sure as hell not me. You two do ten miles before I'm even out of bed." I shiver as a gust of wind whips down the course. I haven't been able to look at his time or splits. I'm too nervous about how he's going to perform today, but he should be making his way to the last two-tenths of a mile any second. "It's disgusting, if we're being honest."

"Holy shit." Rhett shoves his sunglasses in his hair. "Finn is in the top four."

"Top four Americans? That's amazing." I stand on my toes and look up the road, desperate to see him. "He said he'd be happy with the top five."

"No. I mean fourth place overall."

"*What?*" I grab the phone from him and stare at the leaderboard. Finn is behind two runners for Kenya and another from Ethiopia, one of which holds the world record. They're not breaking that today with the difficulty of the course, but to see his name up there makes my heart leap to my throat. "Oh my god. He's going to do it."

The lead car turns onto the final straightaway, and three police officers on motorcycles follow. The cheers from the crowd turn loud, and I stop breathing.

The runner in first place has started to break away and create distance between himself and the cluster of other athletes. I lean to my left and that's when I spot Finn charging through Central Park in third place.

"Let's go, Finn!" Holden screams, and Katarina holds up a sign so he can see us.

I doubt he's going to give us any attention. We're four hundred meters from the finish line and the grimace on his face tells me he's in serious pain.

"Come on, baby!" I yell, and he looks our way. I wave my arms above my head and his mouth pulls into the slow hook of a grin. "Look at him go!"

"What the fuck is he doing?" Rhett asks.

We all watch him veer left, away from the blue line designating the shortest path to the finish line, and toward us.

"Shit. *Shit*. Is he hurt?" I ask.

"He's not hurt, he's—"

Before Rhett can finish, Finn is in front of me. Looping his arm around my neck and kissing me.

"Miss Andrews," he murmurs.

"What the fuck are you doing?" I almost yell. "You have a quarter mile to go and you're in third place!"

"Fuck the placement. I needed to come over and do that." He grins and kisses me again. "See you in a few, baby."

I stare after him as he shoots off to the finish line, still safely in third place. I zip up my jacket and maneuver through the crowd of people, running as fast as I can after him while my VIP access badge swings from my neck.

The announcer calls out Finn's name and I burst into tears, waving the credential to the security guard standing at the finish line. It feels like hours pass before I can squeeze to the front of the media members with their cameras capturing shots of him with the other medalists.

There's an American flag draped over his shoulders,

and when he spots me, he halts his conversation and jogs over.

"You're an absolute idiot," I tell him when he gets close. "Stopping to kiss me like that."

"You're my good luck charm. Wouldn't have felt right if I didn't see you before I crossed the line."

I cup his cheeks and look him up and down. "How are you feeling? How was the race? Oh my god. Finn. Top American and a spot on the podium? You've worked so hard for this."

A fresh wave of tears hits me when I think about the sacrifices he's made. The early mornings where he'd knock out twenty miles before work and the late nights he'd spend in the gym weight training.

When he told me his goal for New York, I believed in him. No one works as hard as him, and seeing him accomplish a dream like this at forty-one is the most special moment in the world.

"I feel good. Puked a little at mile eighteen and the hills nearly got me, but I came out on top."

"Holy shit." I rest my forehead against his. "Third fucking place."

"And sixty-five thousand dollars," he adds.

"You're kidding."

"Nope. Forty for third place and an extra twenty-five thousand for being the first American."

"Maybe I need to start training more seriously so I can bring home some cash. Oh, Finn. You are incredible. I'm so happy for you."

"I love you." He turns his head and kisses my palm. "Thank you for standing in the cold and cheering me on."

"I love you so much. I'd freeze my ass right off for you." I laugh when he reaches over the barricade and picks me up. "And I'm pretty sure I'm not allowed down here."

"Don't give a shit. They can deal with it." He kisses me again, and I don't mind the sweat on his singlet or the poke of the safety pins from his bib, because this is exactly where I want to be. "You know you're going to have to stand at mile twenty-six during every race from now on, right?"

"I'll be there with a huge-ass sign."

"Good." Finn takes off the flag wrapped around his body and hands it off to Rhett. "I couldn't have done this without you, Margo."

"I didn't run twenty-six point two miles. That was all you, buddy."

"You were there, though, and that's what matters."

"I think the only way this could've ended any better is if you wound up in the medical tent. A little role reversal and a full circle moment."

"You're my favorite person in the world," he says, dropping his voice low. "Remember that time you asked something about where we would be on our three hundred night stand?"

"Vaguely. Eleven months is a long time together, Finn, and I've said a lot of things."

"So many things, and I like hearing them all." He reaches past my ear, and his phone is in his hand. "Could you do me a favor?"

"Anything."

"Take a look at this TikTok video and tell me what you think."

"A TikTok—Finn. Are you having a stroke? Since when do you watch TikTok videos?"

"Just watch it, Miss Andrews."

I huff and tap the screen. The video starts to play. It's of Finn, and I turn up the volume so I can hear what he's trying to say.

"Just finished fifteen miles," he says in the video,

wincing as he squats on one knee. "Want to make sure I get this pose right. I'm going to be doing it after every long run so I have it perfect come Marathon Sunday."

"What—"

The video keeps rolling, and there's clip after clip of him kneeling in various places across Chicago. Sometimes he's slower to get on the ground. Other times he's quick, dropping to a knee then popping back up. When the screen goes black, I blink up at him.

"Here's what happens after a three hundred night stand," Finn says to me, and he holds up a bag.

"Is that weed?"

"What?" He bursts out laughing and shakes his head. He moves his thumb out of the way, and I see the flash of a diamond. "Nah. It's something better."

"What is going on?"

"If you can catch me, I'll tell you."

"You know I'm slow as hell compared to you. And you just ran a full marathon. The last thing you need to do is run more."

"Fine. Let's try something else." Finn grins and gets on his knees. He pops a leg up and gestures to the phone. "This is why I've been practicing after every long run. So I can get in the right position and say what I want to say."

"What do you want to say?" I whisper.

"There are a lot of people around, so I'll save the senti-mental part for when we get back to our hotel later. I love you, Margo." He takes my hand in his. "I love you so much, and the only thing I want to do with you is dash all the way down the aisle until you're my wife. Until we've been married for fifty years and you're sick of me."

"That's a lot of one-night stands." I let out a watery laugh and get on the ground with him. "I don't think I can ever be sick of you. Even with your silly jokes."

Finn slides the ring on my finger, and I start to cry again. Never in a million years did I think I'd be at the finish line of the New York City Marathon getting proposed to, but here I am.

With the greatest man I've ever met who's looking at me like he won more than sixty-five thousand dollars in prize money, and I'm on top of the freaking world.

ACKNOWLEDGMENTS

Thank you so much for reading! I've had this idea for a book with this premise since I saw a reel of a runner unsteady on her feet at the finish line of the Boston Marathon. The idea would not go away, so here we are!

If you enjoyed Finn and Margo's story, I'd be grateful if you left a quick review on Amazon and Goodreads! Positive reviews do wonders for indie authors like me!

Thank you to my beta readers who read this quickly after such a fast turnaround from my last book. Your feedback, as always, is so important, and this project would be nothing without your help and insight.

Thank you to all the Bookstagrammers/BookTokers who shout out authors in their posts and videos. You all are truly the heart and soul of the book community. Please know how much your enthusiasm for our work means.

Thank you to Hannah and Britt for your wonderful editing, as always. You two are powerhouses, and I'm so thankful to have you in my corner!

Thank you to M&R. You are my favorites and I love you!

ABOUT THE AUTHOR

Chelsea Curto is a flight attendant who lives in the Northeast with her other half and their dog. When she's not busy writing, she loves to read, travel, go to theme parks, run, eat tacos and hang out with friends.

Come say hi on social media!

ALSO BY CHELSEA CURTO

D.C. Stars series

Face Off

Power Play

Love Through a Lens series

Camera Chemistry

Caught on Camera

Behind the Camera

Off Camera

Camera Shy

Boston series

An Unexpected Paradise

The Companion Project

Road Trip to Forever

Park Cove series

Booked for the Holidays